If ever in your life you are faced
with a choice, a difficult decision,
a quandary,

Ask yourself,
"What would Edgar and Ellen do?"

And do exactly the contrary.

Edgar & Ellen

PET'S REVENGE

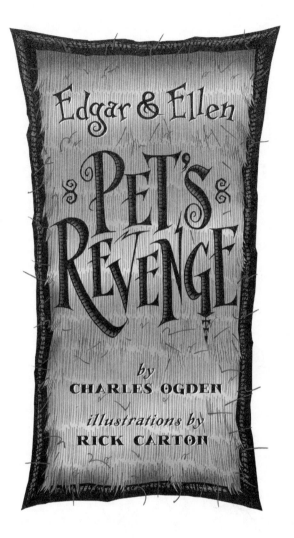

Edgar & Ellen

PET'S REVENGE

by
CHARLES OGDEN

illustrations by
RICK CARTON

ALADDIN
NEW YORK   LONDON   TORONTO   SYDNEY

Watch out for Edgar & Ellen in:

Rare Beasts
Tourist Trap
Under Town

🕯ALADDIN
An imprint of Simon & Schuster Children's Publishing Division
1230 Avenue of the Americas, New York, NY 10020
Text and illustrations copyright © 2006 by Star Farm Productions, LLC.
All rights reserved, including the right of reproduction in whole or in part in any form.
ALADDIN and colophon are trademarks of Simon & Schuster, Inc.

Designed by Star Farm Productions, LLC.
The text of this book was set in Bembo, Auldroon, P22 Typewriter, Brighton, and Cheltenham.
The illustrations in this book were rendered in pen and ink and digitally enhanced in Photoshop.
Manufactured in the United States of America
First Aladdin Paperbacks edition June 2006
10   9   8   7   6   5   4   3   2   1

Cataloging-in-Publication Data is on file with the Library of Congress.

ISBN-13: 978-1-4169-1408-2
ISBN-10: 1-4169-1408-0

HERE IS MY DEDICATION—

Abigail, Nicole
Wise Athenas rescuing
Scribes from wayward words.

Diana, Barbara
Reveling in forge fires like
Iron Hephaestus.

Cary, Erika
Atlases hoisting the globe
With thankless resolve.

—CHARLES

A NETHERWORLDLY SPHERE

A Game of Chase 1

1. A Scenic View 5

2. The Trouble with Pets 10

3. Morella 14

4. A Good Dusting 17

5. Bearskin Twin 21

6. A Crying Game 24

7. Enter the Twilight Zone 27

8. Squeaking By 29

9. Duck, Duck, Goose 33

10. Rodent Trip 36

11. Lawn and Order 37

12. Feeding Time 40

13. Bells and Weasels 41

14. Takeover Makeover 45

15. Deep Cover 49

16. Going Global 52

17. Tour de Farce 54

18. Locked, Shocked, and Abandoned 60

19. Gut Wrenching 62

20. Rise and Outshine 64

21. Stephanie Strikes Back 67

22. Judith's All-Stars 68

23. Slick Thinking 71

24. Hair-O-Dynamics 75

25. Chivalry, Alive and Painting 78

26. Tallyho? 79

27. Duly Noted 81

28. Mineral Water and Old Lace 87

29. You Can Lead a Horse to Paint 91

30. Freaky Clean 95

31. Let the Fun Begin 100

32. Tweezed 102

33. Snap 106

34. Truth Be Told 108

35. Ire Unleashed 113

36. Drink Me 114

37. Attack of the Bones 118

38. False Witness 119

39. Scarred and Feathered 122

40. Mi Dog Casa Es Su Dog Casa 123

41. Just Add Water 125

42. Think Tank 126

43. Seeds of Deduction 128

44. Helmet Head 132

45. A Drop in the Bucket 134

46. Misery Loves Company 136

47. Light Reading 139

48. Send in the Clown. 140

49. Twists and Turnips. 144

50. Showtime 149

51. Sister Dearest 154

52. In Time of War. 160

53. History Repeats 162

54. Downward Spiral. 165

55. Breakthrough. 168

56. The Belly of the Beast 169

57. The New Agenda. 173

A Game of Chase

Swish—swish—swish—swish.

Pet whisked across the floor. The hairy creature sprang and catapulted from a loose floorboard onto a banister. It slid toward the library, just as a butterfly net slammed down behind it.

"Drat! Missed again," growled Edgar. "Sister, Pet's coming your way!"

"I've got it, Brother."

Ellen pulled on a catcher's mitt and crouched at the bottom of the stairs.

Pet flew straight for the glove, but at the last moment, it launched off the banister and landed on a chalkboard eraser, quickly skidding out of Ellen's reach.

"Hurry, it's heading for the kitchen!"

Like a canoe over a rocky waterfall, the eraser tipped over the stairwell and—*thumpa, thumpa, thumpa*—rode two flights down, coming to rest on the stone kitchen floor.

A pot rack hung from the ceiling. Pet looked back: it heard the twins barreling down. Pet hopped onto a chair and then to the table. The frying pan was within reach. Pet jumped....

Too late. The twins tumbled into the kitchen and spotted Pet dangling from the pan by a strand of hair.

"I'll get it," said Ellen. She hurled a plate at Pet.

The plate missed, and as it flew past, Pet dropped and rode it into the dining room. Just before the plate crashed against the far wall, Pet leapt off and landed in a dumbwaiter. A wooden panel slid down, sealing it off from the dining room. Three more plates smashed nearby.

"Help me get that panel up!"

Pet flipped a switch and the miniature elevator escaped, descending two floors to the game and trophy room. When the panel opened, a safari's worth of animal heads glared down from the walls. Pet bounced onto a bare sofa spring and into the mouth of a stuffed boar.

There it waited.

Soon it heard a rattling on the stairs.

"You take the study. I'll search in here." Edgar entered the game room. "Here Pet, Pet, Pet…"

Pet moved not a hair.

Edgar lifted the sofa cushions and glanced into the trophy cups.

Finally, he turned to go. Pet sighed softly. It closed its eye and rested against the front row of boar's teeth.

A loose fang popped out and clattered to the floor.

Edgar spun around. He looked up at the boar's head. Within, a yellow glimmer shone like a cat's eye— or a Pet's.

"Aha!" Edgar triumphantly strode to the boar. As he reached his hand into the mouth, Pet sprung. Bouncing off Edgar's head, it grasped a chandelier with a hairy tendril and swung toward the game room door.

The creature flew through the air, away from Edgar, toward freedom and—

Smack!

—landed in Ellen's catcher's mitt.

1. A Scenic View

Mayor Knightleigh and his wife and daughter stood on the uppermost balcony of the Knightlorian Hotel. Construction was nearly finished, and the family had come for their daily inspection.

"Just think, Stephanie," said the mayor. "Someday, when you are mayor, this will all be yours."

The mayoral daughter sighed contentedly.

"Me, the Mayor of Nod's Limbs," she said.

To the north lay the quaint town of Nod's Limbs, and from where they stood they could see the clock tower, Town Hall, the seven covered bridges spanning the Running River, and even, in the far distance, the ruins of the old Waxworks. It was an excellent vista all around—except, that is, for the western view.

West of the Knightlorian stood a tall house. In basic design it looked very much like the hotel: a mix of brick and stone rising eleven narrow stories, capped with a large round window and a cupola.

But this was where the similarities ended.

The Knightlorian was painted a cheery lavender—Stephanie Knightleigh's favorite color—with spotless green shutters and flower boxes hanging outside the windows. Petunias and pansies lined the front drive, fountains and cherub statues dotted the yard, and rose bushes encircled the building. On the roof, a row of Nod's Limbs flags waved to the rest of town.

The other house did not wave flags. Instead, black iron spikes shot skyward from the roof, and below them, cracked windows encased in gray stone seemed to glare at onlookers. Dingy, broken shutters smacked against the stone walls at the slightest gust of wind, and spidery weeds choked out what little grass grew in the rocky soil. A small, decrepit shed stood in the lifeless garden and appeared to be sinking into the surrounding swamp.

Judith Stainsworth-Knightleigh peered at the view, her lips pressed tightly together.

"Atrocious," she said. "I can't wait until the crew knocks that abominable house down. We'll use the stones to line our driveway, and the rest will make decent firewood."

"You're going to tear it down?" asked Stephanie.

"Of course," said the mayor, thrusting out his ample gut. "Why do you think I built the Knight-lorian to resemble it? Once I present our new and improved replica, the Nod's Limbs Historic

Preservation Society will have no quarrel with demolishing that horror."

"That horror is home to those horrible twins, Daddy," Stephanie said.

"Twins?" Judith glared at her husband. "You told me it was abandoned, dear."

"Who could inhabit such a ramshackle monstrosity? I *thought* it was abandoned," the mayor said.

"Only abandoned of decency," Stephanie quipped.

"Hmm…a minor complication." The mayor stroked his double chin. "Well, we'll find a way to fix this. I always say—"

"Quiet. I'm trying to problem-solve," said Judith. "Yes, I know: a proclamation."

"I love proclamations!" exclaimed the mayor.

"If we can't tear down the awful thing, we'll at least make it less of an eyesore. You will announce the creation of the Nod's Limbs Civic Beautification Committee, to which I volunteer my services as the group's first chairperson. And as chairperson, I choose this house for our inaugural project."

"Brilliant as always, darling," said the mayor.

"Like I say in my book *A Cleaner Home, A Happier You*, with a good scrub, a fresh coat of paint, and some landscaping, any house is salvageable," said Judith. "*Better Homes Than Yours* is currently covering renovations. What better publicity for the Knightlorian's grand opening than to see me on television, restoring the Old World mansion next door?"

Stephanie looked quizzically at her mother.

"The twins will never let you near their house."

"This is a matter of public conscience, Stephanie," Judith replied. "It is for the good of all Nod's Limbs. I will simply talk to the parents and—"

"Mother, I don't think they *have* parents," Stephanie said. "No one has ever seen them—I bet they left because they couldn't stand their nasty children."

"You know these twins?" asked the mayor.

"Know them?" Stephanie said, clenching her teeth. "Daddy, they're the torment of this town! They—they sabotage every parade, every school dance, every ball-game, every *birthday party*! Whenever something goes wrong, they're behind it! Yes, I know them."

"Excellent. If we encounter any resistance, you can convince them of their civic duties," said the mayor.

"WHAT?" Stephanie cried. "Those two are civic *menaces*!"

"Then you're the perfect person to teach them a little community-mindedness, darling," Judith replied.

"It's settled then," said the mayor. "Tomorrow I'll send our official hotel landscaping crew next door to get things hopping!"

Stephanie looked from her mother to her father. Judith patted her hand, perhaps just a little harder than necessary, and Stephanie winced.

2. The Trouble with Pets

Pet lay wrapped snugly in a jump rope on the billiards table in the game room.

"I can't imagine what has gotten into it," said Ellen. "Something must be done about this odd behavior."

"Yes, I prefer the old, slow, stupid Pet," said Edgar, pacing the length of the room. "How do you suppose we can get it back to normal?"

He snatched two badminton rackets from the wall and handed one to Ellen. "You serve."

Pet squirmed frantically, but Ellen ignored this and picked up the creature. "Now, over the past several months, Pet has gotten gradually more active. When exactly did this change begin? What could have triggered it?"

She tossed Pet in the air and served. *Thumph.*

"Do you think the Mason is involved?" Edgar asked. *Thwath.* Pet flew back to Ellen.

Fwumph. She frowned. The twins had tried valiantly to sabotage the building of the Knightlorian Hotel, but their efforts had backfired, thanks to a mysterious foe: the Mason.

Edgar jumped as Pet sailed over his head. *Whumph.*

"The Mason was scared of Pet," Ellen said. "But something else did happen about that time. We found the lab."

In their hunt for the Mason the twins had uncovered a dusty laboratory in a cavern beneath their house. There, row upon row of ancient scientific equipment had lain forgotten for untold years. Amidst it all was a rambling journal that gave clues to a mystery they didn't yet understand.

"Hmm," mused Edgar. "We've caught Pet trying to sneak into the lab before."

Whack.

"Trying to escape!"

Fwack.

Edgar reached up and caught the trussed hairball. He studied it thoughtfully. "If Pet were trying to escape from us all this time, why wouldn't it just slip out the front door or out a window?"

Pet narrowed its eye.

"How should I know?" asked Ellen. "Maybe Pet prefers caverns and sewers. Maybe it finds the stench comforting. We do."

Edgar's eyes lit up. "Stench! There's something else down there with a distinctive smell."

"The balm," said Ellen. "Of course!"

When the twins discovered the secret lab, everything in it was coated with an odorous white film that smelled both sweet and foul, like fruit left too long on the vine. The journal writer called it "balm" and talked about harvesting it for mysterious research.

Edgar put down his racket and lobbed Pet back to Ellen.

"Make sure Pet doesn't get away. I'll bring up something from the lab with balm on it. If Pet reacts, we have our answer."

Edgar dashed off, and Ellen stared into Pet's single eye.

"Don't worry, Pet. We'll soon figure out what's ailing you, and we'll have you back to molasses mode in no time."

Pet wriggled in its bonds, but Ellen held steady.

From the greenhouse below came a crash and the tinkle of scattering pottery.

"Ah," said Ellen. "Morella calls!"

3. Morella

Morella's mother, Berenice, had not been your average placid garden plant, to be sure. Berenice was a carnivore and fed on insects, and when she swallowed them they sizzled in her gullet like bacon fat. Occasionally she mistook fingers or toes for bugs, and because her mouth was lined with hard, pointy, toothlike seeds, she could leave a nasty scar—Edgar's thumb bore the evidence.

Berenice's great misfortune was that she had taken root in the junkyard next door, a site destined to become the Knightlorian Hotel. When construction began, Stephanie Knightleigh herself had planted the shovel that sealed Berenice's doom, and thus was she lost to this world forevermore.

The plant had one last surprise up her fronds, though.

Each night, Berenice's toothy seeds fell from her mouth; by morning, a fresh set had grown in to replace them. Neither Edgar nor Ellen could explain it. Ellen, a budding botanist, had tried numerous times to prod a seed into a seedling. Alas, every attempt had failed.

Except the final one.

Ellen had rescued eight seeds from Berenice's deathbed. Seven produced nothing. But the eighth—planted in a beaker salvaged from the lab—did what its brothers and sisters had failed to do: it sprouted into a healthy green shoot.

This shoot, whom Ellen named Morella, thrived in its beaker and was now a bold, bulbous beauty. And if her mother had been aggressive, Morella was positively vicious.

"Morella!" yelled Ellen, entering the greenhouse with Pet in her arms. "You've thrown another plant to its death. Naughty girl!"

Pet cowered as Ellen pushed Morella to the back of her shelf. Though still small, Morella thrashed in her pot and snapped her jaws with a ferocity Ellen had never witnessed in Berenice. Pet closed its eye and shivered.

Ellen stooped to examine the potted shrub that had, until a moment ago, lived innocently next to Morella.

"My stenchwort! Honestly, when will you learn?" Ellen sighed and stroked the unruly plant. Morella's mouth, yet to sprout its first seeds, clamped onto Ellen's finger. "Hungry again? Well, what do you expect? You reject flies and moths and all the things that are easy to get. How many times a week can a strip of flypaper catch dragonflies and hornets?"

Ellen spotted a hard-shelled beetle crawling out of a floorboard. She snatched it and tossed it to Morella, who caught it in midair. A familiar crackle came from her little green gullet, and the plant settled down.

Edgar burst into the greenhouse carrying a rattling wooden crate. He ducked behind a large blood lily.

"Did you get the balm?" Ellen asked. Edgar did not answer. "Edgar, what are you doing?"

"Hide!" he whispered loudly, squinting through two spiny leaves.

"Hide? From what?" Ellen bent behind a table.

"Heimertz," Edgar said. "I think he followed me from the basement."

Nothing scared Edgar and Ellen like their home's unpredictable caretaker, Heimertz: his looming frame, his ever-present smile, his inability (or unwillingness) to utter a single word. After a chilling encounter with Heimertz during their search for the Mason, neither sibling had a desire to cross his path again.

Ellen poked her head cautiously over the table and surveyed the yard beyond the windowpane. A shadow fell upon her, and Heimertz passed, carrying a patched beach ball under one arm and a duck under the other.

The duck glanced at Ellen and quacked, but Heimertz lumbered on.

Ellen shivered. Her brother emerged from his hiding place and exhaled.

"Well, then," he said, placing the wooden crate on the table. "Let's see what gets Pet ticking."

4. A Good Dusting

Edgar opened the crate. He had tossed in a collection of crusty, dusty scientific implements, flasks, and hand tools, all coated with the odiferous white balm. When spread thin, the balm came off in flakes, but in bigger globs it stuck to the fingers like chewed gum.

As Edgar placed the items on the table, something on the crate caught Ellen's eye.

She wiped off the dust, revealing a faded, peeling label:

Deliver To: Augustus Nod, The Tower
Mansion on Nameless Jane

From: Thaddeus, Foreman, Nod's Jands
Waxworks

Augie—Here are the newest samples of your Nigh-Everlasting Candle. Does this batch meet your standards? —Th

"Edgar, where did this box come from?" said Ellen.

"The lab," said Edgar. "Where do you think?"

"Did you see this label? It belonged to Augustus Nod!"

"*Nod?* As in *Nod's Limbs* Nod?" Edgar asked.

"The 'Tower Mansion on Nameless Lane' must be our house," said Ellen. "Maybe Nod is the stranger who built the house and the lab. Maybe he wrote the journal."

"Hmmm. So Nod built this place and a secret underground lab so he could—do what, exactly?" asked Edgar. "Invent new candles?"

"It does seem like a lot of trouble just for that," agreed Ellen. "But think, we live in a landmark—we can start charging admission. Ancient history is the kind of baloney those goody-goody townsfolk go nuts for."

"I don't want *anyone* from this town waltzing around *my* house," said Edgar. "Anyway, Pet is our primary concern today."

Ellen shrugged and lifted Pet over the table. Pet opened its eye wide, and the ends of its hairs started to quiver.

With Ellen still holding on, the hairball lunged for the table. Its entire mass trembled with a vibration that Ellen felt all the way to her skull. Her teeth rattled.

"Wh-wh-what is it do-oo-ooing?" she chattered.

Pet glided methodically over the tools. Each hair seemed to writhe, and from somewhere inside its tuft came a soft whirring sound, like a buffer polishing the hood of a car.

"Ellen! Look! It's—it's cleaning the table spotless! Pet's true calling: an automatic duster!"

"It's not dus-dusting," said Ellen. *"It's sucking up the b-b-balm!"*

Indeed, not a speck of the balm remained. The flasks, the tools, even the balm specks on the tabletop— everything that Pet passed over—looked spotless, as if the gluey gunk had never been there at all.

Pet's hair poofed out like a porcupine's and its pupil contracted to a pinpoint. With a surge of energy, it leapt over Ellen's head, causing her to lose her grip and smack her fist against her forehead. Pet dashed out the greenhouse door.

"So! Pet *eats* the balm," said Edgar at last.

"Eats it? With what mouth?" asked Ellen, rubbing her forehead.

"The balm must give Pet its newfound vigor. Our feet have tracked the stuff from the lab all through the house—Pet has been feasting on it."

"We need to cut off the little hairball's supply or it might never be the same again."

As night deepened, the twins Pet-proofed their house, securing the lab's secret entrance through a wine cask in the subbasement. While they worked, they sang:

Who knew this balm was such a threat?
We must undo its strange effect,
For every child ought to get
A perfect plaything like a Pet:
It makes a lovely chimney sweep,
Slingshot ammo, a wig for cheap,
A clog for drains—just shove it deep—
A pillow when you fall asleep.
Oh Pet, don't fret, for we prefer
To have you back the way you were!

5. Bearskin Twin

The next morning, as the twins rubbed the sleep from their eyes and straightened their striped footie pajamas (which they wore at all times, even when awake), a strange sound drove away all thoughts of Pet. From the yard below came the clamor of rumbling engines.

"Does Heimertz own a motorcycle?"

"I doubt Heimertz could ride a *bicycle*."

The twins ran to the window. Workmen were attacking their yard with gardening tools. The twins recognized one of them as the head gardener from the Knightlorian.

"It's a *lawn mower*, Edgar! On *our* lawn! Mowing!"

The twins raced down flight after flight of stairs. Edgar threw open the front door and yelled at the man pushing the mower, but the roar of the engine chewed up Edgar's voice along with a thick patch of redroot skunk cabbage. Edgar marched out onto the walkway just as an errant stick flew up from the mower and nearly cracked him in the jaw.

"Hey! You with the lawn mower! Quit vandalizing our yard! You're on the wrong property!" Edgar pointed to the lavender behemoth next door. "That canker of a hotel is over there!"

The man cupped a hand to his ears, shrugged, and aimed the mower at a gnarled hedge. Edgar clenched his fists and stalked toward another worker, a tiny man with a large tank of weed killer on his back. A look of sheer terror spread across the little man's face.

"That's right," snarled Edgar. "Be afraid."

The man stumbled backward, his face pale.

"BEAR!"

He dropped his weed sprayer and fled.

"Bear?" Edgar asked, puzzled.

A shadow fell across Edgar's path, and he turned around slowly.

Ellen, draped in a terrifying but very dead bearskin from the parlor floor, lumbered past him. Growling fearsomely, she chased four screaming landscapers from the yard and down the nameless lane that led back to town.

Once they had disappeared, Ellen returned, throwing off the mangy bear rug.

"Moments like this make life worth living," she said. "By the way, Edgar, just what did you think you were going to do? Yell them away? You're losing your edge, Brother."

"Ridiculous. You didn't give me a chance. I was going to…to…" Edgar paused.

"Disappointing. Very disappointing," said Ellen. She strode back into the house, dragging the bear rug. Edgar followed, protesting. Neither of them saw the purple-clad figure standing at the end of the lane.

Stephanie Knightleigh was not easily discouraged. She did not budge, even when four grown men rushed by her, shouting "Save yourselves!" and "Abandon your weed whackers!"

As she gazed at the dark tower before her, the mayor's daughter only muttered, "I'm telling Mother."

6. A Crying Game

Edgar was standing in the kitchen ladling one-bean broth into two bowls, when he saw a shadow whisk by out of the corner of his eye. He whipped around. The kitchen was empty.

Brandishing a spoon, Edgar dove under the kitchen table. "Gotcha!"

No one was there, either.

He ran out of the room, yelling, "I know you're around here somewhere, Ellen!"

As soon as Edgar left, the pot rack shook, and Pet dropped to the counter.

The creature sidled up to a bowl of broth. In it, Pet could see its own yellow eye peering back.

Suddenly, its pupil started to grow, large and round, until it was nearly the size of the whole eyeball. Only a halo of yellow shone around the enormous black dot, like the moon eclipsing the sun.

From the pupil's dark abyss, a single tear appeared. This grew larger and heavier until it hung, suspended, over Edgar's bowl.

Plop!

Pet wept several tears into the bowl. Then its pupil shrank to normal size, just as the twins entered the kitchen.

Before Pet could scoot under the potbellied stove, Ellen squashed the scuttling hairball beneath a mildew-laden plunger.

Edgar plucked the soggy Pet from the rubber cup. "Join us for supper?"

The twins took their bowls of broth to the dining room, where Edgar climbed onto a chair and hung Pet from a drapery hook.

Ellen devoured her meal right away, but Edgar waited. Pet watched him carefully.

From his satchel, Edgar pulled a halved bicycle inner tube that had a turkey baster pump attached to

one end. He poured his broth into the tube and aimed the tip across the table.

"Sister, say *ahhhh!*" He squeezed the pump.

Splort! A stream of broth arched over the table just as Ellen looked up, her spoon halfway to her mouth. The broth hit her right between the teeth.

"Ack!" Ellen coughed and sputtered as she swallowed her unexpected extra helping.

"You were shoveling down your first bowl so quickly," said Edgar. "I thought you would want more. *Oink oink*, little piggy!"

"Your—days—are—numbered!" choked Ellen.

"The newest weapon in food-fighting," Edgar announced proudly. "I call it the Shovin' Spoonful. You were my test case. It went beautifully, I have to say."

"When you least expect it…when you're fast asleep, I'm going to…to…" Ellen stopped.

"To what? What are you going to do? No ideas, eh?"

Ellen seemed not to hear him. She sat back in her chair and gazed at the empty bowl in front of her. Finally she looked at Edgar.

"Air. Need some air. It's stuffy in here," she said absently, taking her bowl back into the kitchen. Edgar heard her place her dish in the sink. He waited for retaliation, but Ellen did not return.

"Take your time. I'll be ready," Edgar called. He surveyed Pet, still hanging above him.

"Comfortable?"

Pet swayed silently from the hook. It watched Ellen approach Edgar from behind with a full bowl of broth.

7. Enter the Twilight Zone

Too late, Edgar saw the bowl swoop down. He cringed, waiting for the smack of soup upon his head.

It never came.

He opened one eye to see Ellen neatly arranging the broth and a spoon on the table in front of him. She fluffed a napkin and laid it gently on Edgar's lap.

"Eat up, Brother. You very generously gave your soup to me earlier and didn't save any for yourself."

"What did you put in it?" asked Edgar. "Hot pepper? Eggshells? Dead mosquitoes?"

"I didn't put anything in it," said Ellen. "Well, actually, I did add some cinnamon for flavor. Try it. You'll like it."

"Not on your life." Edgar shoved his chair back from the table.

"Will it help if I test it first?" Ellen took a sip. "Mmm…yes, cinnamon does the trick. Edgar, please, before you waste away to nothing!" She held out the spoon.

Edgar cast a wary look at his sister. Not only was she acting bizarrely, her voice sounded strange. It was almost as if she were—Edgar shook his head—telling the truth. Curiosity got the better of him.

Keeping his eyes on Ellen, Edgar took the spoon and swallowed the broth.

She was right. The cinnamon made it quite tasty.

"Ellen, what are you doing? Why are you suddenly concerned with my eating habits?"

Ellen looked confused.

"I—I don't know. I thought it would be a nice—"

Ellen started to gag. Her lips formed a familiar snarl.

"What are you looking at?" she spat at her brother. She seized the bowl and dumped it on his head before storming away.

"That's more like it," said Edgar, licking a trickle of watery soup that dribbled down his cheek. "Ellen, wait up. I've got a great idea to get back at the Knightleighs for their morning invasion!"

He followed his sister, leaving the overturned bowl and puddles of broth on the floor.

Pet's tangled mass of hair writhed, and in seconds the creature was free of the drapery hook. It dropped safely to the chair below, hopped to the floor, and bounced—almost *skipped*—from the room.

8. Squeaking By

That afternoon the twins lugged two bulging suitcases into the empty lobby of the Knightlorian Hotel. Ellen slapped a bellhop cap on Edgar's head, then yanked the elastic cord underneath his chin, letting it go with a nasty snap.

"*Ouch!* What was that for?"

"Just for being you. Now go!"

"And what will you be doing? Lounging about while I do the grunt work?"

"Hardly," said Ellen. "I have other matters to attend to." She handed Edgar an oversized bellhop's jacket and placed a white chef's hat on her own head. "I've cooked up a little plan of my own." With that, she strode toward a set of swinging double doors marked KITCHEN: EMPLOYEES ONLY.

Edgar buttoned up the bellhop's jacket, then hoisted the suitcases onto a shiny luggage cart. He hopped on and shoved off with his foot, riding it until it crashed into the elevator doors.

Inside the suitcases, something squeaked.

Edgar pressed the UP button.

"Patience, little ones. Just a short ride to chaos."

Edgar waited for the doors to open, and too late heard the mayor's laugh booming inside the elevator. There was no time to hide.

"Rides like a charm, doesn't it, sweetie pie? And we got it for next to nothing from a condemned hotel in Smelterburg."

"It rides roughly. Have Eugenia check it."

Judith Stainsworth-Knightleigh stepped out of the elevator first and whacked her shin against the cart. As she gasped in pain, the mayor bumped into her, and she tumbled on top of the suitcases. The bags rippled and stretched.

"My new luggage cart! Err—Judith! Are you all right?"

Mayor Knightleigh reached for his fallen spouse, but she smacked his hand away.

Judith turned to Edgar.

"Who are you, you oaf?" she barked, then frowned at a rip in her stockings.

Edgar glanced at one of the toppled suitcases. A black tail twitched through a tear in the fabric.

"I'm—I'm the new bellboy, ma'am," Edgar stammered. "Just hired yesterday."

"Who hired you?" asked Judith, examining her hair in the reflective elevator doors. Despite her fall, every strand had stayed perfectly in place.

"Uh, that woman in the office. The hiring person who does all the hiring. She hired me, ma'am." Lying on the fly was not Edgar's strong suit; Ellen was the better storyteller. Edgar's palms perspired.

"Now, this young man has initiative!" cried the mayor. "We're not even open for business and he's already lugging luggage—just for practice!" He squinted at Edgar. "You're not on the clock, are you?"

"Of course not, sir."

"Excellent. Work harder."

Judith scanned Edgar from head to footie.

"Ask one of the housekeepers to take that jacket in. You look like an urchin," she said, then marched down the hall.

Edgar smiled. "I'll get right on it."

Mayor Knightleigh nodded and started after his wife.

A loud squeak burst from one of the suitcases. Edgar held his breath. The mayor turned and tilted his head to the side like a cocker spaniel. He walked back to Edgar and rolled the luggage cart back and forth. More squeaks.

A bead of sweat dripped from Edgar's brow and splashed onto the marble below.

"Oil those wheels, young man. A Knightlorian luggage cart mustn't squeak. We shall run a squeakless hotel!"

"Right away, sir."

Satisfied, the mayor followed his wife out of the building.

Edgar waited until the mayor's clomping footsteps faded into the distance. Then he shoved the cart and luggage inside the elevator and pushed the button for the top floor. He cracked his knuckles.

"Going up!"

9. Duck, Duck, Goose

Crispy Aromatic Duck, Braised Sliced Duck, Roasted Cantonese Duck…

Ellen's finger traveled down the menu.

Shredded Goose with Ginger and Spicy Onions, Goose in Plum Sauce, Gosling Knightleigh…

"Now I know what happened to all the birds at Founder's Pond. South for the winter, my pinkie."

Ellen tossed the menu aside and opened the door to the walk-in freezer. Inside swirled a thick fog of cold air.

The icy mausoleum was filled from top to bottom with frozen beefsteaks, pork loins, and lamb shanks. Ellen carefully searched the walls, pushing aside frosty boxes of split chicken breasts.

High on the back wall, behind densely stacked boxes labeled MALLARD, Ellen discovered what she had been looking for: the thermostat. It was set at twenty degrees. A note, and a rather rude one at that, was taped above:

PLEASE DO NOT RAISE TEMP! IF YOU GET
COLD IN THE FREEZER, BUNDLE UP AND
DO JUMPING JACKS INSTEAD.

Ellen despised jumping jacks.

She grasped the thermostat and started to turn the dial.

Suddenly, her arm pulled away and her fingers curled into a fist. Her whole arm shook. She clutched her right wrist with her left hand and forced it forward, but the right arm rebelled again, this time jerking back and knocking her chef's hat to the floor.

"What's happening to me?" Ellen exclaimed.

She whirled around.

"Who's there?"

Ellen shook her head. "It must be the cold. Getting to me. Imagining things. Could be dangerously close to frostbite. Need to do this and get out."

She took a deep breath and lunged for the thermostat with both hands, seizing the dial.

"MUST DESTROY FOOD!"

Her pigtails whipped from side to side, her frame convulsed, and her teeth gnashed, but Ellen's hands would not turn the dial. With a final burst, she rammed the thermostat with her body, attempting to smash it altogether. Her legs buckled, and she collapsed to the floor.

"What am I doing?" she asked, flat on her back. "Why would I want to ruin all this delicious food?"

She propped herself up on her elbows and glanced at the boxes of frozen ducks that had tumbled to the floor during her self-wrestling match. Her eyes filled with tears.

"Poor duckies."

10. Rodent Trip

Alone on the top floor of the Knightlorian, Edgar opened his squirming suitcases. He hopped aside as the pack of rats mushroomed out in all directions.

"Go, go, go!" he shouted. "Show them what happens to those who stir your master's anger!"

In seconds, the rats dispersed down the long hallways into the unoccupied hotel rooms. Edgar chortled and entered the waiting elevator.

"Operation: Squirmin' Vermin complete." He pushed the button for the lobby.

Now, rats are rather predictable creatures. Find them some cozy walls in which to scurry and a modest supply of crumbs to fill their stomachs, and the average rat has no reason to wander afar.

However, rats will not sit around and wait for a well-insulated wall to crack or a hole to form. Nor will they linger patiently inside an empty pantry for crumbs to magically appear.

Rats have noses that are always twitching, bellies that are constantly craving, and tiny, clawed feet that are forever scampering here and there. Rats are rodents of the now, and should one dwelling not provide the warmth or the nourishment they seek, their instincts will quickly drive them elsewhere.

These cold and hungry rats raced across every square inch of the hotel's top floor, but they did not find a single hole nor a solitary crumb of food. They finally converged in the hallway and huddled together, their squeaks unified into one whine of hunger and discontent.

A lean and almost hairless rat ran toward an open door with a red EXIT sign, and the rodent mass followed. The flock of tails and teeth quickly descended ten flights of stairs and pushed through the revolving lobby door.

The lead rat stopped a few yards beyond the front entrance of the hotel and rose onto its back feet. It sniffed the air, then scampered toward the only other building in the area that held the promise of food and shelter.

Like a rodent tidal wave, the rest of the rats chased after, heading straight for the tall, gray mansion next door.

11. Lawn and Order

When Officer Dwight Strongbowe, a thirty-five year veteran of the Nod's Limbs Police Department, retired from the force, he traded in his handcuffs for a hand trowel. His enjoyment of landscaping was equaled only by his affection for chasing criminals. Sadly, throughout his long career, Nod's Limbs had seen not a single felon, so his passion for law enforcement had gone unfulfilled.

Such was not the case for his landscaping interests. The meticulous nature of Nod's Limbs homeowners cried out for around-the-clock vigilance when it came to their lawns and gardens, and Officer Strongbowe answered that cry. After recruiting twelve retired officers and one spunky rookie, he founded Lawn and Order, a team of landscape cops armed with weed whackers, hedge trimmers, and an unwavering commitment to yard care.

Lawn and Order was the most zealous band of landscapers ever assembled, and Judith Stainsworth-Knightleigh was their most fervent patron. She purchased all the equipment for the squadron, and in return she demanded only their allegiance.

Officer Strongbowe's private line rang before dawn on a dew-laden Monday. The former policeman was already awake, drinking a mug of black coffee and replacing the nozzles on his hoses. Judith's orders were clear.

"Yes, ma'am…right away…thank you, ma'am."

Officer Strongbowe made a phone call of his own, and less than an hour later he and his deputy, the gawky rookie Nathan Ruby, rolled up in front of the twins' house on a powerful blue and gray tractor lawn mower. The two men surveyed the yard.

"Wow, Chief," said the rookie.

"Take note, Nate. Won't see one like this again in your lifetime. Good thing the boss called us in."

Officer Strongbowe patted the top of his mower like a cowboy might pat his best horse. He pumped the gas pedal, and the engine neighed. "Ol' Annabelle has her work cut out for her today, don't ya, girl?"

12. Feeding Time

Overnight, the rats worked their way inside the twins' house, swarming into various holes and cracks. By dawn, their twitching nostrils had led them to the kitchen, and they scampered over the floor and countertops in search of discarded crumbs. A *crash* called them to attention.

A plate lay shattered on the stone floor. Above it, on top of the icebox, a mound of hair looked down with a single yellow eye.

The hairless rat ran forward and squealed, then sniffed the icebox.

Nodding its eye, Pet nudged open the icebox door. The rats poured in, devouring every tidbit of food.

The contents of the icebox would not have appealed to even the hungriest of persons, but the moldy cheese, rancid meatloaf, and stale bread made for a rodential feast. When every last scrap was tucked away in their greedy bellies, the rats collected below Pet.

Pet leapt off its perch and landed amidst the furry assembly. It fluffed out its hair and blinked. The hairless rat squeaked again—as if validating some peculiar new alliance—and the rest of the pack echoed with squeaks of their own before dispersing into the walls. Within seconds, the floor was clear.

13. Bells and Weasels

"Sister, wake up."

Edgar poked his slumbering sibling's shoulder. She rolled over, clutching a headless stuffed bear in her arms. Her usually pointy eyebrows now curved gently.

"More…tea…teddy…?" Ellen mumbled, still asleep.

"Get *up*!" Edgar kicked her mattress.

Ellen opened her eyes, blinked several times, and smiled. "Good morning, Edgar!"

"We have trouble!" snapped Edgar, yanking his sister out of bed and dragging her up a ladder to the attic-above-the-attic. There, the twins' telescope poked out through the shingles of the roof. "They're at it again. Seems more of Knightleigh's lackeys have been sent on a doomed mission."

Ellen put her eye to the lens. An army advanced down the weed-choked path and into the front yard. Two men dressed in navy blue overalls led the infantry, riding a mower over jagged stones and dead branches. A row of marching men followed, each bearing a lawn tool. One carried a tree trimmer with a curved blade that glinted in the morning sun like the very sickle of Death.

"Look at all our new visitors!" said Ellen.

Edgar shoved Ellen out of the way. He strained to read the inscription on one of the polished badges.

"Department…of…Lawn…Enforcement. Preposterous!"

But Ellen had already shimmied down the ladder. Then Edgar heard what sounded like the cry of a mortally wounded bird.

Ellen was singing.

Without him.

And the tune sounded happy.

Edgar chimed in as best he could.

Ellen:
The sun is up. The morning sweet
Has brought more strangers to our feet—
We have visitors to greet!
Come on, Edgar, faster!

Edgar:
Who'd dare knock upon our door—
Knightleigh's goons come back for more?
Sister! Wait for me before
You toss out these trespassers!

Edgar chased Ellen's melody through the house. He did not notice the many rats ducking out of sight and, in particular, a striking hairless rat sitting next to Pet in the study.

As Edgar reached the foyer, someone rang the doorbell.

Once pressed, the doorbell did not merely ding or buzz. In a delirious cacophony, hundreds of hidden bells chimed, clanged, banged, and gonged from the uppermost cavities of the house to the depths of the subbasement. Bells, bells, bells! The tintinnabulation of the bells rang with enough force to shake ancient dust from the ballroom chandelier.

Even Edgar, an enthusiast of deafening noises, winced. As the last bell tinkled and faded, Ellen swung the front door open. On the threshold stood Judith Stainsworth-Knightleigh and Stephanie.

Pet arrived in the dumbwaiter, just in time to hear Ellen greet the Knightleighs.

"Welcome, friends!"

14. Takeover Makeover

"Hello, young lady. I am Judith Stainsworth-Knight-leigh of the Lofty Hills Stainsworths and the Nod's Limbs Knightleighs. I am an expert on happier home living, and I have come to help you find the happiness you have lost in this home."

Judith extended her gloved hand to Ellen.

Ellen eyed Judith's white glove, and her even whiter smile. She shook hands.

Edgar gasped.

"Pleased to meet you, Mrs. Stainsworth-Knight-leigh," said Ellen. "My name is Ellen."

Judith brushed off the palm of her glove, but the mark left by Ellen's soiled hand remained. The woman's smile tightened but did not falter.

Stephanie looked suspiciously at Ellen. Though most of the kids in town knew the twins were always up to no good, Stephanie Knightleigh was the only person in Nod's Limbs who could trace all local disturbances back to the pajama-clad twins, whether it was a cheap prank like exploding candles or a sophisticated plot to sabotage the construction of the Knightlorian Hotel. She and Ellen in particular had always sparred, and in recent years, the conflict had grown ugly—as ugly as

Ellen's missing pinkie nail, the victim of a fight involving Stephanie and a claw hammer.

Now Stephanie poked her foot through the doorway and gingerly tapped the floor, testing for booby traps. Judith pushed past her.

"May we...silly me, of course we can."

"Careful, Mother," Stephanie said, "I know her games. I know *both* their games. These twins cannot be trusted."

Edgar stepped between Judith and Ellen. He pointed to the door.

"OUT!"

Ellen, sweet grin plastered to her face, shoved Edgar aside. He tripped and fell over a rusty spittoon. Pet poked out from the top.

"You will have to excuse Edgar. He's been such a grump lately."

Judith walked Ellen farther into the front hall, careful not to touch her grimy pajamas.

"I've seen it before, Ellen," said Judith. "When one spends one's days in a drab house, one can succumb to anxiety, hostility, and eventually deep depression. I call it 'Gloomy Home Syndrome.'" She glanced back over her shoulder at Edgar. Pet ducked back into the spittoon. "Your brother exhibits severe symptoms."

"What do you think you're doing here?" asked Edgar.

"As I am sure you know, my husband is the mayor," Judith said. "And earlier this morning he performed the mayoral task he does best: he signed a proclamation. Then he signed this letter."

Judith handed Edgar an envelope addressed *To the Residents of the House at the End of the Nameless Lane.*

Dear fellow citizens,

No doubt you share my great pride in the wonderful beauty of our fair town. Nod's Limbs is the shining jewel of our region, the coziest nook for three counties—and that's including Ambling Dell and Whistler's Glen! Keeping that rustic charm from getting rusty is Job Number One here at the Mayoral Headquarters.

You'll be pleased to know that to maintain our sparkling appearance, I've appointed my capable wife, Judith Stainsworth-Knightleigh, as the chairperson of the newly formed Civic Beautification

Committee. Even better, your home has been randomly chosen by the CBC to appear on the nationally loved and respected television program, "Better Homes Than Yours." Good for you!

Tomorrow a team of skilled carpenters, decorators, and exterminators will arrive at your door to do all the odd jobs you may have been putting off, such as replacing cracked windows, or trimming the waist-high tufts of ragweed around your front door. Our team is there to be sure everything around your home is in tip-top shape, the Nod's Limbs way.

Too good to be true, you say? Well, just like my great-great-great-great-great-great-great-grandfather, Thaddeus, and all the Mayor Knightleighs who have followed him, I put the YOU in YOU ARE SPECIAL.

Terribly sincerely,
Mayor Knightleigh
Mayor
P.S. Vote Knightleigh!

"What an honor!" Ellen exclaimed.

"I don't know whether to laugh or to *really* laugh," said Edgar. He wadded up the paper and threw it at Stephanie.

"The landscapers who came yesterday may have been laughable, yes," Judith admitted. "Clearly this project calls for my personal attention, and that is what it shall have, with only my best people on the job. When *Better Homes Than Yours* comes to film, they will find a masterpiece."

15. Deep Cover

Judith yanked apart a set of heavy curtains. Light flooded the room, illuminating regions of the entrance hall that had not seen the sun for many years.

Cobwebs riddled every corner, from the floor up yellowed walls to the pocked ceiling. Flies shook in their sticky prisons as spiders crawled toward slivers of shadow.

For a moment Judith could not speak. Stephanie rushed to her mother's side and clutched her elbow.

"See?" she said. "It's horrendous. A waste of our time. We should get out while we still can, Mother."

"Manners, Stephanie," said Judith, shaking her arm loose. "Now, let's have a tour of this diamond in the rough. Will you be my escort, Edwin?"

Edgar's face turned purple.

"My *name*," he growled, "is EDGAR!"

Ellen danced over to Judith.

"Me, me, me!" she shouted. "Let me show you! I'm a great tour guide!"

"Sister, may we have a word?"

Edgar pulled Ellen aside by a pigtail. Normally, such an action would have gotten him a poke in the eye. All he got was a giggle.

"Isn't this exciting, Edgar, dearest?"

"What is with you?" Edgar asked. "Have you any idea what—did you just call me 'dearest'?"

"Edgar, we have a splendid opportunity to show our visitors just how wonderful our home truly is!" Ellen said.

Edgar grabbed his sister's shoulders and shook her hard.

"Our house is plagued with Knightleighs!" he cried.

"Oh my," said Judith. "How barbaric."

"How typical," said Stephanie. She spied Pet sticking up from the spittoon. "And look at the size of these dust balls. I fear this is hopeless, Mother."

"Nonsense. We'll just get bigger brooms."

Ellen looked over Edgar's shoulder.

"Please, Edgar," she whispered. "Not in front of the *guests.*"

Comprehension dawned on Edgar's face.

"Wait. *Now* I get it," he whispered. "How could I have been so blind? *A splendid opportunity.* You've gone undercover! If we charm the Knightleighs with their own brand of false flattery, *if we lure them into our web,* we can take them by surprise when the time is ripe."

"I'm going to paint the parlor rose petal pink!"

"Your commitment is astonishing, Sister."

Edgar released his sister's shoulders, and Ellen straightened her pajamas.

"I'll wait for your signal," said Edgar. "What will it be?"

"Hmm. My signal will be…my signal will be…a hug!"

Ellen wrapped her arms around Edgar and squeezed so hard that his back cracked. Then she skipped up the stairs, waving for the Knightleighs to follow.

Edgar shook his head.

"That is some serious cover."

16. Going Global

Ellen escorted Judith into the map room on the second floor, with Stephanie stepping cautiously behind. Old globes sat on wrought-iron pedestals, and yellowed, curling maps covered the walls.

In the middle of the room, a colossal and very heavy globe hung by a rusty chain just above the floor. Instead of depicting countries like Switzerland, Austria, and France, this globe showed the dominions of the ancient Roman Empire—lands like Cappadocia, Galatia, and Thrace—all jaggedly raised from the surface.

From the doorway Edgar watched the Knightleighs circle the impressive sphere.

"Sublimely gruesome, Sister," he whispered to himself. "One push and that globe will flatten them. Stephanie will have Mount Vesuvius permanently dented into her forehead!"

He waited for Ellen to act. Mother and daughter stood on the side exactly opposite Ellen—the perfect moment—but Ellen simply rocked on her heels.

Edgar tried to get her attention and made a shoving motion, but Ellen didn't notice. Stephanie, however, did.

"Mother, LOOK—" she started.

"Yes, it's a marvelous piece," said Judith, touching

the globe. "I shall have to contact my friends at *Antiques Price Fest*—this could be worth a fortune." Stephanie eyed Edgar warily and guided her mother to a safer spot.

"Come, ladies!" said Ellen. "I can't wait to show you the rest!"

They headed up the stairs. Edgar crossed the room to follow.

Suddenly, the globe swung at him with the force of a planetary wrecking ball, catching Edgar in midstep and lifting him off his feet. He dropped to the ground with a painful *"Oof."*

Stephanie stepped out from behind the swinging ball and stood over Edgar as he tried to breathe.

"I don't know what you two are scheming, but you're not going to get the best of me, *Edwin*. And when your sister tries, she'll be in for a world of hurt, too."

Stephanie left Edgar gingerly rubbing the Cyprus-shaped bruise forming on his belly. He was still on his back when Pet emerged from behind one of the pedestals and scuttled after the others.

17. Tour de Farce

On the third floor, Ellen could barely contain her enthusiasm when she heard Judith's plans to decorate the master bedchamber with silk pillows in lavender and lace.

The fourth-floor game room, Judith said, would make an excellent sitting room—once the hideous animal heads were pulled from the walls and replaced with portraits of famous Nod's Limbsians (mostly Knightleighs) and the shelves now filled with stuffed birds and lizards were replaced with hand-carved busts of important citizens (mostly Knightleighs).

Both Knightleighs covered their noses as they passed the sixth-floor kitchen and hurried up the next flight of stairs.

On the seventh floor, where she found a musty den and an elaborate pipe organ, Judith shook her head in frustration.

"The design of this house is simply bizarre!" she complained. "Severely angled ceilings, useless alcoves that do nothing but collect dust, spiral stairs so steep that they beg a twisted ankle! Surely the architect was a lunatic—who ever heard of putting a kitchen on the sixth floor?"

"His name was Augustus," Ellen chimed in. "Augustus Nod. We think he built our house, as well as the secret—"

"Nod? Well, he *was* a lunatic," said Judith. "But a builder? I think not."

Pet, hiding behind the rusty organ pipes, peered out at the mention of the home's original owner.

"No, we're sure of it! He was performing the most peculiar experiments in the—"

"No more than rumor, Ellen. Nod lost his mind after his wife's death. He did nothing but wander in the woods after that—he most certainly wasn't constructing ridiculous mansions," Judith said as she spied Pet. "Aha. At least you keep a dust mop handy. The next step is using it."

She plucked Pet from the organ and began dusting.

"Hmmm," mused Ellen. "The clues seemed so clear."

"It's embarrassing this town is named after him," Stephanie said with a sniff. "Thank goodness Thaddeus Knightleigh, *my* great-great-great-great-great-great-great-*great* grandfather, was mayor by the time he vanished, and not working in the Waxworks any longer."

"Nod vanished?" Ellen asked. "Where did he go?"

"Who cares? Maybe he left town. Maybe he drowned in the Running River."

Judith shook Pet and let loose a cloud of dust. She waved it away, grimacing. "Well, who better to fix a lunatic's flawed design than myself?" Judith tossed Pet back onto the organ. Her dust rag scuttled off behind the pipes. "Come along, girls."

The next stop was the eighth-floor library.

"Libraries are nice," Judith said. She gazed at the massive oak shelves that housed thousands of old and rare volumes. "But what this house really needs is a home theater."

Judith thumbed through an old tome titled *Morte d'Artur,* then picked up another book with the words *The Peloponnesian Wars* on the cracked leather cover.

"Not even the Nod's Limbs Public Library will want these old books." She shrugged. "We'll send them to the dump, or use them as fuel for the upcoming Bash of the Bonfires festival."

When they stepped into the ballroom on the ninth floor, Judith and Stephanie gasped. Though cluttered with junk, the ballroom was still a spectacular sight.

The expansive room had high ceilings, an intricate chandelier made of a thousand teardrop crystals, and unshrouded half-moon windows that allowed in ample light.

"This is it," said Judith. "With accent furniture, detailed moldings, shantung window treatments, and a marble floor, *this* will be our featured room for the *Better Homes Than Yours* broadcast."

Suddenly, powerful and sinister choral music filled the air—a scratchy rendition of the German anthem "O Fortuna."

"What is that racket?" cried Judith, covering her ears.

"My favorite song ever! Doesn't it make you feel like dancing?" asked Ellen. She grasped Judith's hands. "Come, dance with me!"

Judith looked horrified and attempted to disengage her fingers. Stephanie tried to wrest Ellen away, but Ellen took this to mean that Stephanie wanted to join them, and she threw an arm around the Knightleigh girl.

"Dancing frees the spirit. Doesn't it feel good, Stephanie? Be free with me!"

Panting, Edgar staggered into the ballroom and saw Ellen hugging the Knightleighs.

"The signal!"

Behind the hugging trio sat an open steamer trunk full of carburetor parts and sheets of sandpaper. Edgar lowered his shoulder and ran at ramming speed.

Ellen spotted her charging brother and pushed the Knightleighs out of the way, then kicked out her foot.

"And...dip!"

Edgar somersaulted into the steamer trunk, and Ellen slammed the lid and turned the key. The music stopped as suddenly as it had started.

Ellen spoke sternly into the keyhole. "I am ashamed of this behavior, Edgar. I want you to think about what you've done and how you can become a more pleasant person."

She helped Judith and Stephanie up from the floor.

"I am so sorry about my brother."

"This ballroom is the perfect place to begin my magic transformation," said Judith. "Your disagreeable brother simply won't get any of the credit."

Ellen whispered into the keyhole. "Hear that? No credit for you, crabby britches."

They whisked down the stairs while Edgar pounded and cursed his sister from within the trunk.

Pet sat atop an old phonograph. It scampered in a circle, and the record player's turntable started spinning. Pet rode it cheerfully like a merry-go-round, and the decaying needle dragged through the grooves of the record. The ominous chorus filled the ballroom once again.

"Ellen, is that you?" called Edgar.

A moment later, the hairless rat scurried to the trunk. It squeaked to its comrades. Dozens of rats emerged from behind cabinets and radiators and joined their leader in what looked like a collective rat dance atop Edgar's prison, as if they were celebrating the capture of the person responsible for their suitcase internment.

"Ellen! I can hear you! Let me out!"

Pet leapt off the record player and moved to the stairs as the music slogged to a stop. It gestured to the hairless rat, and the rodents scurried after their leader and his one-eyed collaborator.

18. Locked, Shocked, and Abandoned

Illuminated by light entering chinks in the ancient wooden chest, a photograph of Harry Houdini beamed down upon Edgar. Edgar had long practiced the techniques of the world's greatest escape artist, and he had taped Houdini's picture to the underside of the trunk's lid for inspiration.

"She *knows* I haven't mastered this escape yet, Harry!" Edgar snarled. "Handcuffs first, then straitjackets, *then* trunks!" He leaned uncomfortably on the spare auto parts, and a steel rod jabbed him in the leg.

"Always evaluate your resources, right, Harry?" He winked at the photograph and slid the steel dowel into the keyhole.

The lock was complicated; several hours passed and Edgar had worked through only three of the lock's four tumblers. While he fiddled, he tried to guess Ellen's plans.

"She's spiteful," he muttered. "But Knightleighs are invading our house! And with me in here, she'll have to take them on all by herself."

Edgar remembered Ellen's words the previous day: *You're losing your edge, Brother.*

"Maybe she *wants* to take them on herself," he said. "She's always thought she was smarter because she's older by two minutes and thirteen seconds. We'll see about that—aha!" The lock clicked, and Edgar threw open the trunk lid. The ballroom was bathed in moonlight.

"Behold," he shouted. "Edgar the Escapist!" He stepped out of the trunk, bowed, and blew kisses of victory to an imaginary audience. But a moment later, his face sobered.

"She thinks she can take the Knightleighs single-handedly," he said. "But I too can play the lone wolf game...and I have sharper teeth."

19. Gut Wrenching

Edgar rubbed his aching neck and stood below the trapdoor that led to the twins' bedroom; he could hear Ellen snoring.

He walked to the ballroom window. Down in the yard, six cobalt blue Lawn and Order push mowers sat in a straight line along the uncut northern lawn, patiently waiting to rumble into action at dawn.

"Sleep well, dear Sister," Edgar said. He headed downstairs, picking up his satchel on the way. "Tomorrow you'll see the carnage of Operation: No Mow."

Edgar turned each mower on its side, exposing the vulnerable, metallic underbelly. He pulled a wrench from his satchel and loosened the rotors on the blades.

The scheme was not like the ones Edgar usually conceived and diagrammed step by painfully detailed step. It was a simple prank. Just the sort of thing Ellen would do, only Edgar did it first.

He put the wrench back in his satchel and returned the mowers to their upright positions.

"Feels good," Edgar said. "I think I'm going to like flying solo." He yawned, but a noise behind him jolted him awake.

Standing not ten yards away was Heimertz, and he held one of the lawnmower blades Edgar had just unfastened. The caretaker smiled his toothy grin. His teeth, like the steel he clutched, glinted in the moonlight.

"YAAAAAAAAA!" screamed Edgar, dashing for the front door and forgetting his satchel on the lawn.

Heimertz took an apple from his pocket and ran it across the mower blade, peeling off the skin in one long strip. Then he tossed the blade aside and returned to his shed, munching noisily.

Something rustled in a brittle patch of dead grass near the mowers. A yellow eye peered out, and Pet emerged, stealthily creeping toward Edgar's satchel. It climbed on top of the leather bag and pushed it open.

A moment later, the grass rustled again, and the hairless rat crawled out. It sniffed the air, turned back to the grass patch, and squeaked softly. A dozen rats came forth. Tails, whiskers, and teeth worked in fluid cooperation until the rats had removed the wrench from the satchel. Like ants looting a picnic basket, the rodents carried the tool across the ground and beneath the nearest mower.

Pet scurried over to supervise the work of its minions.

Meanwhile, Heimertz stood at his shed window, chewing his apple core and watching.

20. Rise and Outshine

"Wakey, wakey, wakey, sleepyhead!"

Edgar groaned and swung his fists at the voice.

"I just…went to sleep…." he moaned.

"Rule 14 in Judith's book *Sweeping Your Way to a Better Life:* 'The early bird gets the dust mites!'" Ellen poked her twin with a bony finger, and he jerked upright.

"Leave me be before I tie you up with your own pigtails!"

"Breakfast time!" Ellen said. "Come on, I'll make us pancakes! With strawberries and whipped cream!"

"I'll pancake you." Edgar glared at his smiling sibling. "Still want to play this game, do you? Play on, Sister. Your feeble attempts at psychological torture are futile, and I have bigger fish to drown."

Edgar pulled his sister to the high round window that overlooked the yard below.

"Wait till you see what happens when those lawn morons start their engines," he said.

Nathan Ruby had just arrived for the day. He squeezed the handle of a mower and pulled the cord.

"Here it comes!" said Edgar.

Nothing happened. At least, nothing *bad* happened.

Nathan Ruby steered the roaring mower into the tall grass, leaving a freshly shorn path behind him.

Edgar pressed his forehead against the window.

"I don't understand…those blades…I…"

"You're right, it *is* a beautiful sight." Ellen danced behind him, swinging her headless teddy bear.

"You did this," Edgar hissed. "You sabotaged my sabotage."

"You're sure you don't want pancakes? The icebox is completely empty, so I'm just going to run to the store and—"

Edgar stomped his footies.

"I DON'T WANT PANCAKES!"

Ellen looked at her brother with grave concern.

"Perhaps you should go back to bed, Mr. Grumpy-pants," she said, before prancing down the stairs. "Come, teddy! More cakes for us!"

Edgar just shook his head.

Edgar:
She may think it's hilarious
To play the host gregarious—
What new depths of contrariness
To undermine me twice!

Ellen:
No more messes, no more leaks,
No more rotten food that reeks,
Clear away the cobweb streaks,
And chase away the mice!

21. Stephanie Strikes Back

"Pancakes!" Ellen yelled down the stairs as the two Knightleigh women entered the house. "Get 'em while they're steamin'!"

"Don't eat anything she puts in front of you," Stephanie said.

"You know I would never eat anything as starchy as pancakes, Stephanie," said Judith. "Nor should you."

"She probably put cockroaches in them."

"Young lady, Ellen is making an effort, which is more than I can say for *you*," said Judith. "You do want to appear on *Better Homes Than Yours,* don't you? Enrique Villalobos is coming. The success of this plan depends on your cooperation."

"Yes, I know, I know—wait, Enrique *himself* will be here?"

"He will. So that scraggly ruffian must be perfect on Saturday. Ellen was quite, er, charming yesterday and simply needs a little polishing around the edges. *Your* influence will help that."

"I'll do my best," Stephanie said sweetly as her mother started up the stairs to the kitchen. But once she was out of earshot, Stephanie muttered, "I'm sure Ellen will be perfect. Perfectly rotten. I don't buy her nicey-nice act for a minute."

22. Judith's All-Stars

The floors of the mansion had been neglected for so long that the rooms were only eight feet, ten inches high instead of the original nine feet. Two inches of solid grime accounted for the difference. When Judith saw the state of the twins' home, she knew there was only one person to call for the removal of such catastrophic filth.

The Nod's Limbs Zoo, home to such fine creatures as sheep, squirrels, newts, oxen, catfish, and bumblebees, might not have had the most exotic collection of animals, but no one could deny that the zoo's spotlessness and hygiene surpassed that of many hospitals. For this, Wesley Puddlesby was the man responsible.

With his flabby belly and narrow shoulders, Wesley did not look the type to climb into a cage full of angry chickens (which he did regularly to maintain the zoo's "What Am I Eating for Breakfast?" exhibit), yet the noble man would risk all manner of bites, pecks, and stings to keep his cages clean. No creature, be it mammal, fowl, or fish, had ever created a mess that had bested Wesley Puddlesby. But then, he had never cleaned up after creatures like Edgar and Ellen.

Wesley Puddlesby eyed the hallway.

"You don't need a hose, Mrs. Stainsworth-Knightleigh," he said, shaking his head. "You need a jackhammer and a blowtorch."

"Leave your sarcasm with the chickens, Wesley," snapped Judith.

"Sorry, Mrs. S-K," he said, and he went to fetch his cleaning products.

Jill Geronimo, of Jill-of-All-Trades Carpentry, arrived shortly after. As always, she wore her special tool belt. It held a hardware store's worth of screwdrivers, hammers, wrenches, and drill bits, and with it wrapped around her waist and over her shoulders, Jill looked like an odd-job bandito.

Stephanie and Ellen stood at the door to welcome her.

"Hello, Ms. Geronimo," said Stephanie. "Why, what a lovely belt. Is that suede?"

Ellen glanced at the journeywoman's belt and spied a claw hammer hanging from it.

Her eyes widened. Her lips quivered. She reached a trembling arm toward the belt.

"Hammer...hit...purple...girl..."

Jill Geronimo caught Ellen's hand and shook it hard. A big smile snapped back on Ellen's face.

"Uh...hi, Ms. Geronimo, I'm Ellen!" she said. "Call me Ellie."

"Pleasure's mine, Ellie." Jill Geronimo marched after her employer.

"I saw that!" Stephanie hissed at Ellen. "You were reaching for that hammer."

"Stephanie!" Judith called. "Come!"

"I'm watching you, *Ellie.*"

Stephanie found her mother in the ballroom, pacing in front of Wesley Puddlesby and Jill Geronimo like a general in front of her troops.

"You are the front line of this intense battle, Wesley," Judith said. "I am counting on you to fight through the filth, to set the stage for a most glorious transformation."

"Of course, Mrs. S-K!"

Judith turned to her carpenter. "Jill, the walls in this ballroom are in deplorable condition. I need you to make them presentable."

"Well, ma'am, I suspect your biggest problem is structural damage," said Jill Geronimo. "I suggest we start by shoring up the—"

"The ballroom," said Judith, gesturing around her. "It looks a mess. This is the proper place to start."

"But if the integrity of the building remains compromised—"

"The *ballroom*, Ms. Geronimo."

Jill tightened her lips in disapproval, but she marched upstairs nonetheless.

"Bad attitude on that one, Mother," said Stephanie.

"It is always a burden to be the only one with vision," Judith said, sighing.

23. Slick Thinking

Per her mother's instructions, Stephanie was supervising the cleaning out of the twins' freezer. She wore a nose plug and goggles. Ellen pulled out a bucket filled with something frozen and brown.

"*Ew.* What is that?" asked Stephanie.

"Grease," said Ellen. "Edgar uses it to cause accidents on festival days."

"I knew it," Stephanie snarled. "I *knew* you were behind the float pileup at the Parade of Picnic Baskets."

"Oooh, wasn't that a charming day?" asked Ellen. "All the willow reeds and wicker!"

Stephanie gazed at the grease, then her eyes fell upon the kitchen stove.

"Hmmm, yes." She gingerly took the grease bucket from Ellen. "What could we possibly do with all this…this…*wonderful* grease?"

"I don't know," chirped Ellen. "What?"

Stephanie set the grease on the stovetop and turned on the gas. A small blue flame jumped to life.

"We'll warm up this grease to…uh…oil the wheels on the new portable buffet for the dining room. We don't want any squeaks to disrupt your first banquet, do we?"

"Of course not," said Ellen.

"Right. So I'll go get the buffet, and you stay here— *by yourself*—with the gooey, melty, messy grease."

"Okay!" said Ellen.

Stephanie pretended to exit to the dining room but stopped just outside the door.

Ellen stood at the stove, stirring the grease and humming.

Stephanie heard footsteps on the stairs, and soon Edgar appeared in the kitchen.

"What fancy meal are you cooking now?" he asked. "Cream of carrot soup? Asparagus stew?"

"I'm melting grease," said Ellen.

"Well, it's about time! Who do you want to slime with it first? That home*wrecker*, Judith? You probably want to nail Stephanie, huh? Well, I'll turn a bucket on—"

"Don't you touch Judith. Or Stephanie. I won't let you near them," said Ellen, pointing a greasy spoon at Edgar.

"I see," said Edgar. "So it's war, then? Fine by me. We'll see how far you get working on your own."

He stomped off.

"Confound her," Stephanie whispered. "Why won't she take the bait?" She strode back into the kitchen.

"Where's the buffet? This is almost melted," said Ellen.

"Oh, I…ah…couldn't find it. We'll do it later," said Stephanie. "But now you can take down those repulsive animal heads in the trophy room. Mother wants them gone before the painters get here."

"Great!" said Ellen, and the two girls headed for the fourth floor.

When they were gone, Edgar stuck his head around the door.

"No sense in letting perfectly good grease go to waste," he said, and he nabbed the bucket of warm goop from the stove.

Edgar climbed the stairs to the ballroom. He passed Wesley Puddlesby scrubbing away at the den floor.

Scrub, scrub, scrub.

Scrape, scrape, scrape.

Scour.

Nothing. The dirt surrendered not an inch.

"Golly," said the zoo janitor. "This is some tough grime."

Edgar scowled and proceeded up the stairs. He met Jill Geronimo on the way.

"I don't care what she says," the journeywoman muttered. "If the stairs *collapse* while people walk up them, this redecoration will be for nothing." She pulled her hammer from her belt and went to work bracing the stairs.

When he reached the ninth floor, Edgar looked from the bucket to the stairwell he had just climbed and smirked.

He found a yardstick lying on the floor and stirred the grease, churning it into a buttery sludge. He worked alone—but something was watching.

24. Hair-O-Dynamics

Pet sat in the middle of the attic floor. The ladder leading to the ballroom was pulled down, and Pet could see Edgar below. While Edgar stirred the grease, it hurried to a pile of scrap material collected from the old junkyard.

Pet rummaged through the dumbbells and telephone receivers and shredded neckties until it found what it was looking for.

A kite.

It was a kite the twins had used many times: Edgar had attached a small harness to it, and he and Ellen liked to strap Pet in and launch it off the roof.

Pet dragged the kite to the opening in the attic floor. Edgar stood at the steps leading down to the library with his bucket of melted grease. Pet crawled into the harness and leaned over the edge of the opening. It closed its eye and pushed off.

Swoosh! Pet swooped down—for a moment it seemed it would nose-dive to the floor below. But the kite caught air, billowed out like a sail, and took flight. Pet opened its eye, and, with a slight shifting of its weight, steered the zooming craft straight for Edgar.

Edgar was holding the bucket, ready to pour, when he heard a sound behind him.

"*Aiee!*" screeched Edgar as Pet flew at him. The kite clipped Edgar's ear, and slammed into the wall. Pet landed upside down on the floor, and Edgar tripped over the shaggy pile. He fell backward and stumbled into the dumbwaiter shaft, dumping the grease all over himself.

The dumbwaiter itself may have been too small for the twins to use, but the shaft in which it traveled was just wide enough to accommodate a scrawny body like Edgar's, especially when that body was covered in grease.

Edgar knocked and bumped down several floors. Finally, the shaft narrowed and Edgar came to an abrupt stop. He twisted and squirmed, trying to reach a door just inches below, but to no avail. He was stuck.

Edgar heard footsteps in the room beyond. The shaft door slid open, and Ellen stuck her head in.

"Good grief, Edgar. So *that's* what all the noise was about. You really need to read Judith's book *No Room for Etiquitters.* It's very bad manners to leave grease prints all over the house," she said.

"Just get me out of here," Edgar grumbled.

Ellen took Edgar's hands and pulled. Edgar spilled

out into the trophy room and landed on top of his sister.

"Disgusting!" Ellen disengaged herself from her brother's oily limbs. "Judith wants this house spotless, Edgar!"

"What's the big idea, Sister, launching the Pet kite at me like that?" Edgar shot back. "Why are you working against me when our combined efforts will oust these intruders?" He pointed a finger in Ellen's face. "If I didn't know better, I'd say you *wanted* the Knightleighs here!"

Ellen grabbed Edgar's finger and twisted it, forcing him to his knees.

"Judith's book says not to point!" she yelled.

Edgar stared incredulously at Ellen. "What has gotten into you?"

"The spirit of cleanliness and good posture," Ellen replied. She released Edgar's finger and stood up straight and tall. "Of taking pride in one's home and improving one's person."

"They've *brainwashed* you," said Edgar.

"Yes, Judith has taught me to wash everything," said Ellen, and she sashayed out of the room, leaving Edgar dazed on the floor.

The sound of hooves and a trumpet blast pierced his glum contemplation.

The painters had arrived.

25. Chivalry, Alive and Painting

Chip Meyers, master painter and amateur jouster, specialized in the painting of maypoles, lances, and shields, and he had founded the Gallant Paintsmen to travel to Renaissance Fairs far and wide. As a bow to historical accuracy, Chip had anointed himself Sir Malvolio, and his squires, Sir Horatio (formerly Hank), Sir Gionello (formerly Tad), and Sir Geoffrey (formerly Jeffrey), had followed suit. Despite their eccentricities, they were superb color consultants, and Judith Stainsworth-Knightleigh was their biggest patron.

The Paintsmen arrived at the house on horseback. With dozens of fresh paint cans roped across their horses, the four noblemen sat silently in their saddles, gazing at the house's gloomy exterior.

Finally, Sir Malvolio unsheathed a long, sleek paintbrush from a leather scabbard and held it aloft. The soft bristles blew in the gentle breeze.

"Good Knights of the Brush, are ye prepared for battle?"

The three men pulled similar brushes from their scabbards. Holding them high, Sirs Horatio, Gionello, and Geoffrey swung their weapons of coloration in frenzied circles, shouting words like *glory*, *majesty*, and *mutton*. The horses huffed and kicked dirt up from beneath their hooves.

Sir Malvolio led the charge to the front door.

"To the paint! Tallyho!"

26. Tallyho?

Edgar looked out the window at the ridiculously garbed painters below and slapped his forehead.

"Oh, come on! These clowns are just *asking* for it."

Then he saw her. Ellen was greeting each of the painters with a curtsy. She tried on Sir Malvolio's hat and crossed brushes with Sir Horatio in mock sword-play. Giggling, she led the absurd crew into the house.

There comes a time when, under moments of extreme stress, the human brain exhibits the amazing ability to ignore the most obvious things around it. A man swimming in shark-infested waters may, as the circling dorsal fins draw ever closer, think to himself, "The water sure seems a bit chilly today."

This is because the true function of the human brain is to carry on, to convince the body to keep slogging forward despite all outward signs that doing so is fruitless. Once a brain gives up hope, the rest of the body can pretty much pack it in too.

Edgar's brain was certainly no quitter. When he saw Ellen cavorting with the painters—without the slightest hint of malice or mischief on her face—he backed away from the window.

"Yes, more intruders. Time to get back to work," he said. "Hmm. The house sure seems a bit chilly today."

Edgar took up a sheaf of paper and a piece of charcoal from a nearby drawer and began to draw up a plan.

An hour later, the charcoal was no more than a nub, and a pile of crumpled papers littered the ground at his feet.

"I don't need you, Ellen!" he yelled. "Do you hear me? I DO NOT NEED YOU!"

27. Duly Noted

Judith patrolled the house in a cheerful mood. The sound of hammers, saws, and paint mixers filled the air. She paused where Stephanie was supervising Ellen as she polished brass doorknobs.

"It's starting to come together, girls, can you feel it?" Judith asked. "I sense a ratings blockbuster for *Better Homes Than Yours*—you missed a spot by the keyhole," she added, glancing at Ellen's work.

"Oh, yes," said Stephanie. "Enrique will be so impressed." She leaned against the wall, right into a spider's web. "Ugh! It's like this house resists cleaning."

"Perhaps your attitude is what's resistant, dear," said Judith. "Filth cannot simply be wished away. It must be washed away. Scrub, scour, polish, and the beauty beneath will shine through. Right, Ellen?"

"Yes, ma'am!"

Stephanie looked over at Ellen, who worked with gleeful fury.

"Some filth goes deeper," she muttered.

"I've been thinking about new details to elevate the natural glamour of this house," Judith said, pacing and waving her hands. "Little things can make a big difference. Something like...well, all the new homes in Lofty Hills have wine cellars in the basement."

"Ooh! We have giant wine casks," said Ellen. "Down in the subbasement—"

"The *subbasement*?"

"I think she means dungeon."

"Want to see it now?" asked Ellen.

"Yes," said Judith. "Show me immediately. Original wine casks—this is the kind of architectural feature that *Better Homes Than Yours* can't resist."

Ellen led them to the basement door. But not only was the door locked, a note had been tacked to it:

OFF LIMITS!

Judith snatched the card off the door and tossed it aside.

"Oh, Ellen, when will your brother cease this childishness?"

"Girls do mature faster than boys," said Ellen as she opened the locked door with a violent kick.

She flicked the switch, but no lights came on.

"That's odd," she said.

They peered into the darkness and saw a glint of white at the foot of the staircase.

"What is that?" asked Judith.

The stair creaked, and the white object came nearer.

It was a toothy smile.

Stephanie, who had once encountered this smile in the depths of the Black Tree Forest Preserve, cowered behind Judith. They could hear lumbering footsteps ascending, and Heimertz's enormous frame took shape from the shadows. The caretaker halted near the top step, whittling a bar of soap into a little lump with a fish-boning knife.

"You must be the caretaker Ellen's told me so little about," said Judith. "If you'll excuse us, we were just on our way to the basement."

"Hello, Heimertz," said Ellen. "He doesn't speak, but what superb oral hygiene!"

Judith frowned. "I must say, sir, after seeing your handiwork here, I think you'd really benefit from my book, *Take Care of Your House Before It Takes Care of You*. Why don't you run off to the bookstore for a copy, and I'll give you a free autograph?"

Heimertz didn't budge, nor did he cease smiling. Instead, he bent down and stabbed the OFF LIMITS!

card with the point of his knife. He held it out for her to see.

"I don't think you understand," Judith said. "I am in charge of the home renovation, and I need to have access to every—"

Heimertz wagged the note in front of Judith's face.

"See here," scolded Judith. "That's rude. Now step aside."

"Hark, what is this wailing I hear?"

Sir Malvolio and his crew strode into the foyer, long-handled paint rollers in hand.

"M'lady, doth this man bother thee?"

"He won't remove himself," said Judith. "The nerve!"

"Sir, you should know better than to insult a lady while the Gallant Paintsmen are near," said Sir Malvolio. He sized up his massive opponent, the sharpness of his blade, and gulped.

"Let us not fight. Simply give the lady passage and we shall part friends."

He brandished his paint roller like a staff, though it trembled in his hands.

Heimertz stood like a statue.

Edgar tiptoed into the room to observe the commotion.

"We have no quarrel with you, good sir knight," continued Sir Malvolio. "But if you will not make room for the ladies, I...I shall make it for them."

With Sirs Horatio, Gionello, and Geoffrey huddled behind him, Sir Malvolio slipped the long handle of his roller between Heimertz and the wall. He began to wedge the giant man aside.

Then things started to happen.

Heimertz dropped his knife and wrested the paint roller from Sir Malvolio's hands. The painter took a swift roller bump to the chest that sent him sprawling. A sharp *tack-tack-tack* sound followed, and the remaining painters found their own rollers knocked from their grips.

In a sequence of upward swings, Heimertz dealt the three men wide streaks of Magna Carta White up their tunics and faces.

"See the madness in that shimmering smile?" cried Sir Gionello.

"Aye!" shouted Sir Horatio. "A feral knave is he!"

"I have paint up my nose!" yelled Sir Geoffrey.

Heimertz slammed the roller onto the floor and pushed it forward like a steamroller.

"Forsooth!" yelped Sir Malvolio, and he scuttled backward like a crab. Heimertz advanced on the group, spinning and thrusting his roller erratically. The Paints-men scrambled out the front door, yelping and crying for mercy.

Heimertz dropped the roller and returned to the basement, closing the door behind him.

"Yes. Well. We'll look at the wine casks another day," said Judith.

28. Mineral Water and Old Lace

Ellen watched Wesley Puddlesby as he took a jack-hammer to the kitchen floor. She reached for a bottle of mineral water, the kind Judith was always drinking, and as she did so, she touched something hairy next to the bottle.

"Pet! What a surprise," Ellen said, looking down. "Have you been drinking my mineral water?"

Pet paused, then nodded. Its pupil, which had been enormously wide, was shrinking to its usual size. A potent tear dripped to the floor, unnoticed.

"Of course you have. Everybody enjoys the sparkling coolness of mountain lakes!" She patted Pet, and it leaned into the affectionate rub like a cat.

Ellen took a deep, hearty swig of the water.

"Ah," she said. *"Refreshing."*

She pressed a button on the new intercom. Jill Geronimo had disabled the makeshift system Edgar had cobbled together from tin cans and hoses and in its place installed a modern electronic panel that allowed Judith to bark commands on a whim. This time Ellen did the barking.

"Judith! Stephanie! Where *aaaare* you?"

"I hate these things. Now there's no place to hide," Stephanie said, glaring at the intercom. She stood in the ballroom, which was now full of paint trays, brushes, and tunic-wearing Renaissance men.

"JUUUU-DITH! STEHHH-PHANIE! I HAVE SOMETHING TO SHOOOW YOU!"

Judith strolled up to Stephanie.

"One can only hope she washed her outfit and wants to model it," she said. "Did you tell her to come up?"

"Oh, uh, just about to," said Stephanie. She pressed the intercom buzzer. "We're in the ballroom, Ellen."

"Stephanie, that reminds me. I want you to invite Ellen to your sleepover tomorrow night."

Stephanie tripped over a paint can.

"W-w-what?" she stammered.

"Really, Stephanie, you must be more careful," said Judith, frowning at the spilled paint. "Anyway, Enrique has just informed me that we're doing a *live* show. There is no room for mistakes. Inviting Ellen for a slumber party will give you a chance to help the little scamp with her social skills."

Stephanie could only bite her tongue as her mother turned to the painters.

"Ah, Malvolio! I was not convinced King's Custard Yellow was the right choice for the trim, but you have proven your intuition yet again."

"You are too kind, m'lady," said Sir Malvolio, bowing. He lifted a key ring of paint swatches and fanned them out like a deck of cards. "Perhaps my lady would care to select the color for the eastern wall? I thought perhaps Hey, Nonny Nonny Green or Burnt Stake."

"Neither—make it Madrigal Sky," Judith answered. "I want the sensation of perpetual sunrise in this room."

"Truly, you are a gifted decorator, Lady Stainsworth-Knightleigh," the painter said. He kneeled, kissed her hand, then turned to the other painters. "Good Knights of the Brush! M'lady has chosen Madrigal Sky! What say you?"

The men clacked their paintbrushes and rollers in approval.

A minute later Ellen appeared. Her pajamas were not noticeably cleaner, but they were fancier.

Ellen had attached lace cuffs to her sleeves and collar, and she had sewn colored beads and flower appliqués over the threadbare parts of the fabric. The effect was that of a gaudy patchwork quilt.

"Oh, ah, very nice," said Judith. She elbowed Stephanie.

"How…vintage," Stephanie said.

"Ellen, Stephanie has something she would like to ask you," said Judith. Stephanie gritted her teeth.

"Would you…like…to spend the night…at my house?"

"Oh, I would love to!" said Ellen. "I've never been invited anywhere before!"

"That's…so hard to believe," said Stephanie, trying to smile pleasantly.

"We'll send a limo for you on Friday at six," Judith said. She glided away to check on Jill Geronimo's progress with the marble flooring.

"My goodness, whatever shall I wear?"

"How about a straitjacket?" said Stephanie.

"What?"

"Listen, Ellen, you may have fooled my mother, but your little sham doesn't fool me—not even this rag bag Halloween costume you've got on. Don't think I don't know you're going to unleash some horrible plot once you're in my house."

"I love Halloween!" Ellen exclaimed. "Next year I'm going to be a fairy princess bride!" She danced off after Judith.

"The Bride of Frankenstein, maybe," said Stephanie.

29. You Can Lead a Horse to Paint

True to their Renaissance ways, Sir Malvolio and his men had spent the evening under the stars, camped out on the rough terrain of the twins' front yard (made markedly more civilized by two days of Lawn and Order's "Maximum Sentence" treatment).

Sir Malvolio called to his comrades as the sun appeared over the eastern hills.

"Rest, ye merry gentlemen, is over," he said. "We have walls and walls to gloss ere we sleep again."

"Right-ho," said Sirs Horatio and Gionello.

Sir Geoffrey rubbed his backside. "My butt hurts."

The Gallant Paintsmen entered the house, too consumed in their medieval banter to notice the length of twine that ran from the bridle of Sir Malvolio's horse, Viola, into the house and up the banister.

Once they were inside, Edgar emerged from behind a tractor. He untied a can of Serf's Cap Crimson from

Viola's saddle and, hoof by hoof, dipped the horse's feet into the paint. Then he waited.

Having finished in the ballroom, the painters had moved to the fourth-floor study. They poured out their hues and readied their brushes. The fumes were strong, but Jill Geronimo had installed a high-powered ceiling fan the day before, and Sir Gionello turned it on. The blades began to spin, circulating the air and diffusing the paint vapors but also, unbeknownst to the Gallant Paintsmen, reeling in the twine that traveled down the stairs, out the door, and tugged on Viola's bridle.

At her unseen master's command, the horse trotted toward the house. Edgar raced ahead of Viola and hid in the hall.

As the horse neared the front door, Pet scooted out from under a newly planted shrub along the front walk, the bald rat clinging desperately to its back. Pet somersaulted forward—rat in tow—and the two of them tumbled like a small, fuzzy boulder. After three swift spins, the rat let go and the momentum flung him through the air.

The rat snagged the twine in midair and began to gnaw with the speed of a hedge trimmer. Viola snorted and shook her head vigorously, and before the rat could chew through the cord, it was hurled from the twine into a decorative urn by the stair.

On the front lawn, Pet's mound of hair deflated.

Inside, the voice of Sir Malvolio floated down from the fourth floor. Viola's ears pricked forward. Urged on by the sound of her master and the pull of the rope, she sped up the stairs, knocking Wesley Puddlesby, who was polishing a chandelier, from his ladder and sending Jill Geronimo dashing for cover. She clop-clopped up the stairs to the study, a path of red hoof marks in her wake. Having found her master, she whinnied and stamped.

"Alackaday!" yelled Sir Gionello.

"Zounds!" cried Sir Horatio.

"Aw, geez," muttered Sir Geoffrey.

Sir Malvolio ran after his horse.

"O, fie!" he shouted. "What hast thou done, ye surly nag?"

The Paintsmen chased the horse down the stairs, yelling oaths all the while. Even more horrifying than the mess of hoof prints, however, was the look on Judith Stainsworth-Knightleigh's face when they met her in the front hall.

Edgar peeked out of the closet.

"Make way for out-of-work painters," he said, snickering.

"Sir Malvolio, how did that animal get into the house?" Judith demanded.

"M'lady, please accept our most humble apologies. I cannot explain the brute's perilous deeds," said Sir Malvolio.

"That red, all over the floor," Judith said. "I was about to make a terrible mistake."

"What dost thou mean, m'lady?"

"I nearly had *salmon* carpets installed, when this *red* is the perfect complement to the sunrise scheme of the upper rooms! We'll get carpets just this shade."

"Then—then there is no harm done?" asked Sir Malvolio.

"In fact, the horse has saved everything," said Judith.

A wretched gurgle came from the closet.

"I must have Jill check the plumbing again," said Judith. "And one more thing, Sir Malvolio. If that horse gets in again, you'll be jousting for position in the unemployment line."

30. Freaky Clean

Ellen returned to work with the Knightleighs, but Edgar slogged back upstairs, dazed and exhausted.

Ellen:	Edgar:
Joyous day, an invitation!	*Wretched day, and fresh frustration!*
Time for fun and celebration,	*Our one hope: collaboration—*
What could dampen my elation—	*What has caused this transformation?*
The very air excites me!	*Why does Ellen fight me?*
How our home glitters, good as new	*How can my sister misconstrue*
A wondrous spectacle to view	*The foul intentions of that shrew—*
And this night's delights, all due	*That this plight, this blight is due*
To Judith Stainsworth-Knightleigh!	*To Judith Stainsworth-Knightleigh!*

Edgar sat down on the new floral daybed in the map room. "I can't take it anymore! Not when we should be working together—not with Pet behaving so strangely. I've got to win her back."

Edgar spent the rest of the day planning an evening of fun and games for himself and his sister. He arranged ropes for their treacherous game of hide-and-seek ("hide-and-seek-and-subdue" might have been a more appropriate name), set up minicatapults on either side of the dining room for their traditional slop-slinging competition, and even tried to secure Pet for a round of See Pet Bounce. The creature, however, was nowhere to be found.

Edgar strained the juice from a pickle jar to make Ellen's favorite drink. He left the mug on the kitchen table and went in search of his sister. She was in none of her usual places—not the den, not the game room, not even her greenhouse.

While passing the parlor on the fifth floor, however, Edgar heard a peculiar noise. He crossed to the adjoining room—what was once a lady's bedroom—and heard running water coming from the bathroom.

Edgar flew to the door and banged on it.

"Ellen! Ellen! Are you okay?"

The door opened a crack and Ellen popped her head out. With her came a cloud of steam and a pungent, honeyed aroma.

"Do you mind?" asked Ellen.

"What are you doing?" replied Edgar, wrinkling his nose.

"What does it look like I'm doing? I'm taking a bath."

"But…*why*?"

"Judith insisted."

"What is that horrible smell?" he said, gasping.

"It's not horrible. It's 'White Gardenia and Cassis,'" Ellen said. "Judith gave me some bath beads to try. Now please, Edgar, I do have to get ready. Stephanie's personal chauffeur will be here soon to take me to the Knightleighs."

"WHAT?"

"Didn't I tell you? It's my first slumber party! So be a love and fetch those heels from the costume trunk in the attic, will you? With a little polishing, I think those old shoes will be charming." She slammed the door.

Edgar reeled from the shock. Ellen was actually *attending a party* at Knightleigh Manor, the home of her archenemy and the seat of everything she and Edgar despised about Nod's Limbs.

" 'Chauffeur?' 'Heels?' *'Charming?'* " he repeated. He heard Ellen turn off the tap.

"You can get your own grubby shoes to go with your own…rotty…stench!" He stormed off.

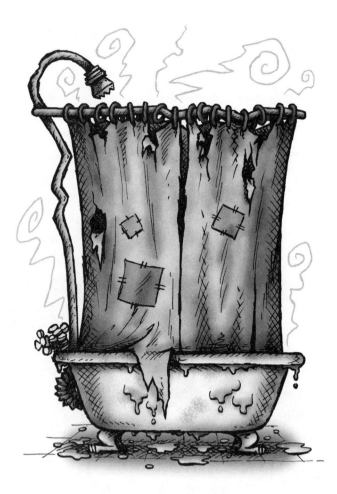

Ellen had scarcely begun to remove the many layers of dirt caked upon her skin from so many days without a proper washing, when a polite beep from outside the window made her jump from the bubbly, albeit browned, bathwater.

"Goodness! The limousine!"

She toweled off, slipped on her pajamas, and fled from the bathroom, tripping on a pair of shoes in front of the door. Edgar had, in fact, brought down the heels. He had also painted a bloodred skull and crossbones on each of them.

"What a prankster," Ellen laughed, shoving her footies into the heeled shoes (the extra material helped them fit perfectly).

Edgar stood in the kitchen and heard his sister *click-clack* down flight after flight of stairs, followed by the sound of stumbling, a shriek, and the unmistakable *clunk* of a body hitting the floor.

"I'm okay!" Ellen called up.

"Break a leg!" Edgar shouted back.

The front door slammed shut.

31. Let the Fun Begin

"You invited *who*?" Cassidy Kingfisher screeched through the phone.

"Don't get me started," Stephanie replied. She paced the floor of the living room and drummed her nails on the phone's receiver. "My mother's making me."

"She's a freak and a menace," said Cassidy. "I still have the bruise from that human bowling prank. Stephanie, she is not welcome tonight."

"That's tough, Cassidy. She's coming. And as long as my mother is looking, we're going to be nice to her. Got it? Ugh, there's the doorbell now."

"Already?"

"Yes. My mother wants me to coach her on make-up before the TV broadcast tomorrow."

"Better start with hygiene first," Cassidy said with a laugh. "Have fun *bonding*."

"See you in an hour. And don't even *think* of stranding me."

Stephanie hung up the phone as Mrs. Munions, the Knightleighs' housekeeper, ushered Ellen into the living room.

"Miss Stephanie…your, ah…*guest* is here."

"Oh, joy." She glared at a smiling Ellen and folded her arms. "Tell anyone you spent the night at my house and I will deny it."

Judith appeared in the doorway.

"Why, hello, Ellen! Don't you look—"

Despite Ellen's best efforts to scour them clean, her pajamas remained dull and worn, the original red and white stripes no more than rusts and grays. Her face, scrubbed for the first time in months, revealed an unsettling paleness, and she wobbled in her heels.

"Don't you look...happy to be here," Judith said. She tugged Stephanie by the elbow and whispered, "You know what to do. Curl that hair, pluck those eyebrows. And that *skin*...salvage it."

Stephanie's cheeks reddened.

"Yes, Mother," she answered and beamed. "You know you can count on me."

"Good girl." Judith squeezed her daughter's shoulders. "Ellen, pay attention to Stephanie tonight, and you will do wonderfully tomorrow on *Better Homes Than Yours.* You must look every inch the gracious hostess. And what is our motto?"

"Stand up straight; walk with poise; don't wear corduroy, it makes noise," said Ellen by rote.

"Precisely." Judith glided from the room, and Stephanie's smile vanished.

"This is so exciting!" Ellen exclaimed. "When will the others be here?"

"Not soon enough. Now take off those shoes before you rip a hole in the carpet. That Lambston Brothers wool is worth more than you are."

Ellen moved to the couch.

"No," Stephanie warned. "You'll stain the leather. Just sit on the floor."

Ellen sat and flipped off the heels.

"So what do we do first, Steph?" Ellen asked, rubbing her footies. "I've never been to a slumber party before."

"I can't imagine why," Stephanie replied. "Maybe it's your close resemblance to the bogeyman."

"Ha! You're funny. Does this mean you want to tell scary stories now?"

Stephanie sighed. "First I give you a makeover. That will be scary enough."

32. Tweezed

Stephanie sat down in front of her longtime nemesis with a basket full of cosmetic accoutrements: lip gloss, a small tub of rouge, mascara, eyeliner pencils, a pair of tweezers, and a dozen or so hair curlers.

"What kind of game is a 'makeover,' Stephanie?" asked Ellen eagerly.

"This is no game," snapped Stephanie. "My mom wants me to…to *beautify* you before the shoot tomorrow."

"Make me beautiful?" Ellen sat up straight.

"Talk about impossible. Why not ask me to breathe through my eyelids?" Stephanie took the tweezers and leaned in.

Suddenly Ellen lurched forward and wrapped her arms around Stephanie.

"Oh, thank you! You are such a dear friend!"

Stephanie wrenched herself free from the tight embrace.

"Enough!"

Ellen shrunk back and pouted. Stephanie gritted her teeth and stared Ellen down like a panther sizing up a piglet.

"What's your plan, Ellen? You've been a mutant since the day you were hatched. Why start playing human all of a sudden?"

Ellen blushed. "It just feels nice being nice!"

"Right," said Stephanie. She leveled her face with Ellen's. "Look into my eyes."

Ellen blinked and tilted her head, confused.

"Look into my eyes, Ellen."

Ellen sat up straight, opened her eyes wide, and looked directly at Stephanie.

Stephanie moved in with the tweezers and plucked a black hair from Ellen's left eyebrow.

"Ouch!"

"Well, then," Stephanie began. "If you really have changed and want to be my friend, there are a few things you need to get straight."

She plucked another hair, and Ellen let out a tiny yelp.

"First of all, I am at the top of the friend ladder. Cassidy Kingfisher is my *best* friend, so she occupies the rung just below me. Clear?"

"Ouch!" A stubborn hair above Ellen's right eye fell to the wool carpet. "Gosh, beauty sure is painful." For

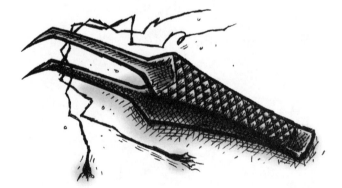

a moment, her voice turned raspy, and she mumbled to herself:

"Painful…pain…tweezers up her nose while she's sleeping…"

"Ellen! *Understand?*"

Ellen shook her head as if snapping out of a dream.

"Oh…um, friend ladder…got it."

"Good." Stephanie dug her fingers into the rouge and smeared color on Ellen's cheeks.

"Now, Heidi Birchbeer and Pepper Poshi are on the next rung, and Neely Gulati is between them and the Huggle sisters. Neely dropped off the ladder altogether when she ran against me for class president, but she fell in line rather well after the crushing defeat, so I might bump her up a rung."

"Can I be on the Huggle rung?"

"No," Stephanie said. "You start at the bottom and work your way up. And you are at the very bottom. Even below Gertie Turkle."

She rolled a curler into Ellen's hair.

"How do I move up?" Ellen asked.

"By doing what all friends do." Stephanie rolled in another curler. "You do what I tell you."

"Is that all? No problem," said Ellen. "So am I beautiful yet?"

"Not yet. Can you believe it?" Stephanie reached for the mascara and muttered, "It's like trimming a dead Christmas tree."

33. Snap

Threatening thunderclouds rolled across the sky, but the impending storm could not compare to the raging tempest that was Edgar, and the kitchen was the eye of his hurricane.

He stalked across the floor, flinging forks and spoons against the wall. When he ran out of flatware, Edgar tossed eggs at the defenseless icebox, then heaved an iron kettle through the window. Finally, he collapsed to his knees.

Head tilted upward, arms outstretched, Edgar unleashed a barbaric wail:

"BETRAYAL! OH, FOUL TREACHERY!"

Thunder sounded in the distance, and winds lashed the old pines of the Black Tree Forest Preserve. At last Edgar's tirade subsided. He sat on the cold kitchen floor, motionless.

Then his eye caught a slip of paper on the kitchen table. The words on it were in Ellen's handwriting, though her usually jagged scrawl seemed smoother now. Each *i* was dotted with a smiley face.

"*Dear Edgar,*" the note read. *"Try not to miss me too much this evening! Feel free to use my bubble bath should you decide to bathe (I recommend it). Also, I have been grooming Pet lately, and the little darling sure seems to love it! Could you give it a thorough brushing before bed? Well, play nice until I am home tomorrow for our big show! Lovingly, Ellen."*

When Edgar looked up, Pet was staring at him from the kitchen doorway. Edgar stood, crumpled the paper, and pointed at Pet accusingly.

"You…"

Edgar caught a glimpse of a lavender hairbrush underneath the tufts of unusually well-groomed hair. He took a step toward Pet.

"Yes, I'll brush your hair, Pet. It'd be a shame if there were any…*tangles*…"

Normally, if Edgar were advancing on it with such malice in his eyes, Pet would cower or slink away as quickly as possible (which, until recently, was not very quickly at all).

But today, Pet neither cowered nor slunk. It stayed right where it was. It rose up on its tendrils, and its pupil zoomed in and out, daring Edgar to come closer.

Edgar hesitated. He'd never seen Pet's eye do that.

The eye shrunk back to its normal size, and Pet zipped away.

Edgar shook his head and breathed in the cool air that blew through the broken window.

"I can't do this alone," he said. He cracked his knuckles. "Sister, you are coming home where you belong."

Edgar ran down the stairs and out the door. He looked north, where the lights of Knightleigh Manor shone in the distance.

As Edgar marched into the oncoming storm, a yellow eyeball glimmered in the small circular window of the twins' attic bedroom.

34. Truth Be Told

At last Ellen's usually scraggly mane fell to her shoulders in loose, lovely curls. Her cheeks finally had a healthy glow, and her eyes sparkled. Ellen gazed in the mirror, barely recognizing herself. Stephanie stood back to assess her work and smiled, pleased with the transformation she'd performed.

Judith peeked in to inspect Ellen's progress. "What do you think?" asked Stephanie. Her smile vanished when she saw the look on her mother's face.

"Oh, no, no, no, Stephanie," sighed Judith. "What did I teach you about hair styles for the angularly jawed?"

"But, Mother, I'm not finished with—"

"Have you learned nothing from me?"

"Look what I have to work with!"

"Stephanie!" Judith said sharply. "A Knightleigh does not make excuses!"

Stephanie drooped.

Ellen continued admiring herself in the mirror.

"I love it!" she exclaimed. "Stephanie, you did such a good job! I've—I've never looked better!"

Stephanie looked at Ellen, and just stopped herself from giving her a smile.

"Well, Ellen," Judith said, "that might be true. But tomorrow you go on live television. Thousands will be watching. *Better* isn't good enough. I need you to look *perfect*."

"I will, Mrs. Stainsworth-Knightleigh," Ellen confirmed. "Steph will make sure I'm ready. Right?"

Stephanie nodded.

"Of course, Mother—"

Judith shook her head. "I don't have time for mistakes," she said. "I had better fix this myself."

Judith simply blotted Ellen's lipstick and pulled her hair back off her face.

"There. *That* is the right look," she said, satisfied.

"I like Stephanie's way better," said Ellen.

"Hmmm…that's why neither of you is leading this project," said Judith. Stephanie watched sullenly as her mother left the room.

"Of course you know best," she muttered, then she turned on Ellen.

"Why did you do that?" Stephanie demanded.

"Do what?"

"Defend me. I don't need anyone to defend me."

"Isn't that what friends are supposed to do?"

"Friends?" said Stephanie. "What do you know about friends?"

The doorbell rang.

"The girls!" cried Ellen, anxious to show off her new look.

Mrs. Munions opened the front door and Cassidy Kingfisher, Heidi Birchbeer, and Pepper Poshi shuffled into the house in silence. Heidi and Pepper waved haltingly at the newcomer, surprised by her new and almost attractive look, but Cassidy ignored her and flopped onto the divan with a dramatic sigh.

"Uh, Ellen," said Stephanie, "you probably know everyone here…"

"Yes, we have met on occasion," said Ellen. "Run into each other in the halls, that kind of thing." Cassidy clenched her fists.

"Easy," Stephanie said to Cassidy. "Okay, let's get this over with. We always play games first. Let's begin with Truth or Dare."

"Ooh! I *love* dares!" Ellen exclaimed.

"I dare you to jump in the pool with rocks in your pockets," Cassidy said, equally brightly.

"Okay!" said Ellen. "You come too, Steph—we can practice synchronized swimming!"

Stephanie scanned the other girls. They looked at her expectantly. She hesitated.

Cassidy tapped her foot while Heidi and Pepper exchanged concerned glances.

"I wouldn't swim in the same *ocean* as you," Stephanie spat.

The girls smiled and relaxed.

"And anyway, we're going to start with truth. You know what truth is, don't you? It's the opposite of everything that comes out of your mouth."

"Truth," Ellen murmured. "Truth. I think I can do that…"

"Tell me, Ellen, who do you have a crush on?" asked Stephanie, grinning wickedly.

"This should be rich," said Cassidy, leaning back against some pillows.

Ellen's cheeks turned pink.

"No one," she said, staring at her feet.

"She's lying—it's called *truth*, Ellen," said Cassidy. "You *have* to tell us. Otherwise you're disqualified."

"But you'll tell everyone!" said Ellen.

"Of course we won't," Stephanie said. "You can trust us."

"Okay, okay," said Ellen. "Don't tell anyone, but...I really superlike...Richard the Third."

Pepper gasped. "Richard Cardigan the Third? You can't like him! I like him!"

"He's in my algebra class. What a dreamboat." Heidi sighed.

"No," said Ellen. "Richard the Third. The hunchback king of England. He killed his nephews to ensure his grip on the throne. My kingdom for a handsome rebel!"

The room fell silent.

"Oh. *Him*," Stephanie said at last. "Great. Fine. On to dares, then."

35. Ire Unleashed

The dark clouds advanced steadily northward over the Black Tree Forest Preserve. Flashes of lightning tore the night, followed by cracks of thunder.

Edgar tramped up Copenhagen Lane, approaching the security lights of the mayor's family compound. As always, he carried his satchel.

"Befriending a Knightleigh...spoiling perfectly good pranks...a *bath* for criminy!"

His grim determination led him to the gates of Knightleigh Manor, which were eight feet tall and topped with spikes. But the bars that were meant to discourage and deter any would-be intruders only fueled Edgar's resolve. He scaled the iron fence and hopped down onto perfectly manicured grass.

"No wall too high, no security too tight, no slumber party too giggly," he vowed.

Then Edgar heard the most unwelcome of sounds to an intruder's ears: a dog barking and racing closer.

Edgar rooted through his satchel, searching desperately for anything that would fend off a vicious canine. A deck of cards, playing spoons, a handheld radio. The only decent weapon was a rolling pin pilfered from Buffy's Muffins. Edgar pulled it out and looked up.

Standing not six feet away was an enormous mastiff. Drool dripped from its fangs, and it gave a low growl.

Edgar raised his rolling pin and prayed it would be over soon.

36. Drink Me

"Let's start with a classic," said Cassidy. "This dare is called Mystery Milkshake, and you have to drink whatever I put in front of you."

"I accept," said Ellen.

"Then on to the kitchen," said Cassidy.

The Knightleigh Manor kitchen was like most of the house: vast and spotless. Glass cabinets rose twenty feet to the ceilings, forcing Mrs. Munions to wheel in a ladder to reach the good china. There was enough counter space for a dozen chefs to cook at once, plus three ovens, four sinks, and two refrigerators with padlocks to keep the mayor out after midnight.

Stephanie wrapped a dishcloth around Ellen's eyes, then sat her at the table.

"No peeking," she said.

The girls joined Cassidy at the counter across the room. She dumped a can of creamed spinach, a handful of dried peas, ketchup, horseradish sauce, pickle juice, and green jelly into a blender.

"Probably needs something sweet," Cassidy said. She pulled out a box of butterscotch instant pudding and shook the powder into the mix.

"But not too much," said Stephanie. "Ellen's sweet enough as it is, don't you think?"

"You guys," whispered Heidi, "won't she get sick?"

"Yeah," added Pepper. "I don't think we should make her drink that."

"You're missing the point," Stephanie said. "What's

a dare if it isn't *daring*?" Heidi and Pepper stared at the floor and said nothing.

"Besides, she can always say no." Cassidy searched through the spice cupboard and removed a bottle decorated with flames. "Hot sauce! Just the thing."

Cassidy hit the Puree button on the blender, then poured the concoction into a tall glass. They placed the glass on the table in front of Ellen.

Just then, Judith entered the kitchen. Stephanie grabbed the Mystery Milkshake and handed it to Pepper, who stashed it behind her back. She glanced around guiltily.

"Good to see you girls again," Judith said. "Are you enjoying yourselves?"

"Oh, yes, Mrs. Stainsworth-Knightleigh," said the guests in unison.

"We were just about to give Ellen a special treat," said Stephanie, patting Ellen's shoulder. Judith eyed the blindfold.

"Ah, yes—Mystery Milkshake. Always amusing," said Judith. "See, Ellen? When you make an effort to fit in, you're rewarded with this kind of friendship."

"Absolutely, ma'am!" said Ellen.

"Excellent. Now, don't overdo things." said Judith, leaving the kitchen. "Remember, two of you have to go on live television tomorrow."

Cassidy took the glass from Pepper and placed it in Ellen's hands.

"Here you go, Ellie," she said. "Enjoy!"

With the blindfold tightly fastened, Ellen could not see the gray, chalky liquid or the lumps of coagulated powder and floating peas. The girls giggled and gagged as Ellen put the glass to her lips and sipped.

"Mmmm," she said. "Is that pickle juice I detect? Yum!" Ellen took a big swig and pulled the blindfold off. "Oh, it looks just like a mud shake I made for my brother once. Tastes a lot better, though!"

The girls gaped at Ellen.

"No way," said Cassidy. "No way *that* is any good."

"Yes, try it," said Ellen. She handed over the glass, but Cassidy pushed it away.

"Not likely," she said.

"No, really, it's good!" Before anyone could stop her, Ellen shoved the glass in Cassidy's face and tilted her head back. Cassidy swallowed a mouthful before she had a chance to resist.

"BLEEEEECCCHHHH!"

Cassidy spit the drink all over Ellen and ran choking to the bathroom to wash out her mouth.

"Maybe she has a weak stomach," said Ellen, wiping the gray glop off her pajamas.

37. Attack of the Bones

"Prepare for battle, mongrel!" shouted Edgar, lurching at the dog.

The beast leapt and hit Edgar squarely in the gut. They landed in the grass, and Edgar waited for the teeth to sink in.

They didn't. Instead, the dog stood on top of Edgar and bit into the free handle of the rolling pin. Edgar read the dog's brass tag: BONES.

Bones tugged hard on the rolling pin, and Edgar nearly lost his grip.

"Let go! This isn't a bone, you dunce!" Edgar twisted out from underneath the dog and managed to wrestle the utensil away. Bones instantly sat at attention, staring only at the rolling pin.

Edgar cautiously waved the item back and forth. The dog followed it closely, then wagged its tail.

"You—you want to play *fetch*?" asked Edgar. Bones wagged his tail again.

Though reluctant to give up his only weapon, Edgar heaved the rolling pin with all his might. Bones took off at top speed.

The rules of fetch ensured that the dog would soon return. Edgar ran as fast as he could to the house.

38. False Witness

Lightning flickered deep inside the storm clouds, but still no rain came. Above the whistling of the rushing wind, Edgar heard a sound more horrifying than a dog's barking.

Laughter.

Not just any laughter: it was the kind he heard only at the most grotesquely joyous festivals in Nod's Limbs. It was the kind of laughter he and Ellen had ridiculed for years, the kind of laughter that pushed the twins to greater heights of mischief.

Edgar skidded across the perfectly shorn yard, following the noise to the back patio. It was there, through the French doors, that Edgar saw the most terrifying sight of his life.

Feathers filled the air. Edgar fought to see through the flurry of fluff. And then, bouncing on a cream leather couch, a tall skinny girl came into view, and it was from her that the repulsive laughter came.

It was Ellen, or what had once been Ellen.

Edgar could excuse the smiles, and the new hairdo, and even the preposterous shoes. But what he saw at that moment was beyond forgiveness.

Ellen wore brand-new pale purple pajamas with lace trim. When Stephanie ran across the room, trailing a cloud of feathers, Edgar saw that she had on a matching pair.

Edgar stumbled back, raising his arm to block the gruesome scene, as a vampire shields itself from sunrise. He shouted to the high heavens, but his voice was lost in the howling wind and booming thunder.

"Gone. She's gone!"

The clouds that had menaced the town for hours finally broke open, and rain poured down in sheets. Edgar staggered as he ran, his eyes blinded by the driving rain, his mind tortured by his sister's betrayal.

> Purple, ruffles—she's insane!
> Some madness courses through her veins!
> That laughter, laughter sears my brain,
> What fiendish forces twist her?
> What slight and sickly memory—
> Would let her befriend Stephanie?
> My blood becomes my enemy—
> And I have lost my sister.

39. Scarred and Feathered

The pillow fight began innocently enough, with the girls playfully decking one another until feathers flew. They got so caught up in the fun that, for a short time anyway, most forgot the misfit among them.

But then Ellen nailed Pepper so hard that her glasses spun off her face.

Ellen laughed hysterically, caught up in the heat of battle. She wore a fresh pair of flannel pajamas, on loan from Stephanie after the Mystery Milkshake fiasco. Ignoring the girls' protests, she whomped around the room, shrieking a hideous war cry.

> *Feathers fly, so duck or die!*
> *(Sorry, Pepper, 'bout that eye!)*
> *Like falling snow the fluff swirls by*
> *In downy jubilee.*
> *Swing your hardest, take a shot,*
> *Show me what your pillow's got,*
> *My friends, you have most bravely fought,*
> *But you're no match for me!*

SMACK! on top of Heidi's head.
THUD! into Cassidy's stomach.

RAM! BAM! Pepper hit the floor.

"I win! I win!" Ellen screeched.

Stephanie was ready for Ellen's attack, and as the enthusiastic pillow fighter lunged at her host, Stephanie stepped aside, opening the French doors leading to the patio. Ellen stumbled into the rain, and a very wet Bones leapt into the room, rolling pin in mouth. Stephanie quickly closed the doors and locked them.

"No, I win."

40. Mi Dog Casa Es Su Dog Casa

Miles Knightleigh, Stephanie's nine-year-old brother, stood at the front door, calling into the storm.

"Bones! Here, Bones!"

He put his stubby fingers to his lips and tried to whistle, but only drooled on himself.

"Bones!"

The dog was nowhere in sight, so Miles marched into the rain, fuzzy slippers and all. He plodded across the lawn toward a large doghouse and shone a flashlight into it.

"Come, Bones," Miles called softly. "You can sleep in my room."

A metal bowl rattled inside, and Miles heard kibble roll across the floor planks. He pushed the flashlight in farther.

Ellen peeked out.

"YAA!" cried Miles. He fell on his bottom into a puddle.

"Hi!" Ellen smiled and crawled out of the dog-house. The rain had caused her makeup to blur into a ghoulish mask.

"Wh-wh-what have you done with Bones?" Miles cried.

"Your cute little puppy dog?" Ellen said. "Oh, he's inside with Stephanie."

"He is? What are you doing in my dog's dog-house?" Miles asked, still sitting in his puddle. "You're not a dog."

Ellen stood and extended a hand. Miles reluctantly reached out, and she yanked him off the ground and onto his feet.

"We're playing hide-and-seek, I think," Ellen said. "Isn't this a great hiding place?"

"But Stephanie's asleep," Miles said. "I could hear her snoring. Nobody's looking for you."

"Ha!" said Ellen. "I win again!"

"She never finds me either."

Wet and cold, Miles looked back at the house.

"I have a bunk bed," he said, turning to Ellen. "I was saving the bottom one for sleepovers. You can sleep there if you want."

Ellen beamed. Two clumps of makeup slid off her cheeks and plopped to the sopping ground.

41. Just Add Water

Halfway down Copenhagen Lane, Edgar stopped running. As he slogged the rest of the way home in the pouring rain, a passing truck splashed by, soaking his pajamas. When he finally reached his front door, he had never been wetter in his life.

On the landing leading into the kitchen, a tarnished full-length mirror hung on the wall. Edgar stared at himself.

He looked paler and scrawnier than usual, dirtier and grimier and—he closed his eyes—alone. He stood like this until he heard a familiar rustle from the kitchen.

Edgar peeked around the corner and saw Pet shimmying across the kitchen floor. It didn't notice Edgar as it hopped onto the table. Then something remarkable happened.

Pet hovered over the mug of pickle juice, and its pupil grew larger than Edgar had ever seen. Edgar didn't move. What could Pet possibly be doing?

In a moment he saw.

A single tear rolled down Pet's eyeball and plopped in the cup, then a second and third. Pet was *crying* into the mug.

Ellen's mug.

"WHAT ARE YOU DOING?" Edgar screamed.

Pet looked up, stunned.

"Get away from there, you monster!" Edgar ran at the creature, but Pet was too quick. As Edgar lunged, Pet dove off the table and between Edgar's legs. Edgar tried to follow, but he tripped on his heavy, wet pajama footies and sprawled on the floor. Pet slipped down the banister and out of sight.

"Villain!" Edgar bellowed. "Wretched beast! You've poisoned my sister!"

42. Think Tank

"Think, Edgar, *think*!"

As he paced the kitchen floor, Edgar gibbered to himself. A thorough search had not revealed Pet's hiding place.

"Pet has been *poisoning* Ellen—changing her. But why now?" he asked. "Why did it wait all these years to strike? We've been mean enough to it—if Pet *could* have done it before now, it *would* have. Which means it couldn't until *now*. Yes, yes—it can do *lots* of new things now, can't it?"

He cracked his knuckles.

"The *balm*. That poison in Pet's eyes—I wonder if it comes from the balm."

He stopped his pacing and ran down the stairs.

When he reached the subbasement, he flipped a latch on a large oak wine cask and its lid swung open. He felt his way down a staircase to an electric generator and cranked it. A string of bulbs crackled to life and the darkness retreated, revealing a vast cavern. It was filled with rows of cobweb-covered tables upon which dozens of scientific implements sat rusting and crumbling.

The old journal was where Edgar had left it: wedged under the leg of a rickety table.

"Now, Augustus, give me something to work with."

43. Seeds of Deduction

Many of the journal's entries detailed experiments performed on the balm, accompanied by charts of numbers and scribbled mathematical equations. Complicated phrases leapt out at Edgar—"electrical impulse simulations" and "mucilaginous breakdown effects"—and soon his eyes glazed over.

Several entries appeared in a bizarre code:

Pilosoculus made an interesting observation today that bears further thought:

"Useless," said Edgar. He rubbed his eyes. "Come on, Edgar, stay focused."

He turned again to the beginning. Several pages in, he found this:

1 May

Another piece of this mystery has been revealed—again, my genius prevails! I have been bedeviled by the mysterious insect-devouring plants in the woods. I have given them the scientific name <u>Nepenthes sinestra</u>, yet from whence have they come? Why do the seeds not sprout in my care?

"Hmm...Ellen had the same trouble with Berenice's seeds," said Edgar. He read on.

I have guessed that it is no mere coincidence that such odd vegetation would live near the Balm spring. Indeed, today my conjectures have proven correct! Having brought a bucketful of Balm from underground, I ladled a small amount onto the cluster of plants on the forest floor. They are, of course, mere flora—and yet I would swear that their little jaws seemed to lunge for the Balm like nestlings for worms. Next, I will mix the substance into soil, and again attempt to plant a seed.

"Ellen planted Morella in a balm-encrusted beaker," breathed Edgar, "and it sprouted!"

He paged forward, looking for more mentions of the plants, and found:

19 January

Dearest Agatha, should you ever return to me and take over the Waxworks from your old father, you must understand the secret that makes our candles so exceptional: The Balm! It is not enough to know that the Balm has powerful effects on one's attitude—

filling one with a virtuous, honorable outlook on life—but you must also understand how to control it. There exists an antidote that lessens the extreme feelings of righteousness (reducing them to mere notions of well-being and contentment), but it also calms the flammable nature of the Balm. The seedlings of N. sinestra are the key! Witness: The Balm nourishes the roots of the plants, which in turn drop seeds that exhibit the exact opposite properties of their nurturer. O Ingenious Nature, author of such divine paradox!

"Morella's seeds!" cried Edgar as he slammed the book shut.

He ran to the greenhouse and found Morella, her fronds writhing as if she were hungry, or angry, or both. She sensed motion in the room and opened her jaws in hopes of catching dinner.

What Edgar saw made him wail.

"No seeds! How could I forget? She doesn't have seeds yet!"

Indeed, Morella had only just sprouted a single woody nub in the dead center of her upper lip, the mere beginnings of her first seed. But the rest of her traplike mouth looked like a baby's gums.

"It could take weeks—*months*—for seeds to fall," grumbled Edgar. "I don't have that kind of time. I need fertilizer, something that will speed up growth. I need...a powerful substance...I need...*tears.* With a few tears, Pet changed my sister overnight. Let's see what they do for Morella."

44. Helmet Head

Back in the laboratory, Edgar scraped up the very last of the fetid flakes of balm and climbed the stairs to the remodeled ballroom.

He pulled old telephone wire through a suit of armor, tossed the wire over the chandelier, then hoisted the armor up until it hung high over the center of the room. Below the medieval snare, Edgar placed the balm.

He switched off the lights, took hold of the wire, and hid behind the steamer trunk.

A yellow eye appeared moments later. Pet glided

across the floor toward the malodorous mound. It gave a soft *puff* as it approached, as if excited.

Edgar's arms trembled under the weight of the armor, but he held fast.

The *puff-puff*ing intensified. Pet's black pupil dilated as it strained to see the prized substance in the dark. Closer, closer…

Pet stopped. Its eye flitted about. Edgar's aching fingers released the wire, and Pet looked up to see the armor plummeting down. The creature darted sideways just as the trap crashed to the ground next to it.

Pet glared at Edgar, then raced for the door.

"Get back here!" Edgar hollered. "PET!"

Edgar scooped up the helmet and sprinted after his prey.

"STOP!"

Edgar dove and smashed the helmet down on the escaping creature.

He slammed the visor shut, locking Pet securely inside. The sad yellow eye pushed against the visor's slats; the helmet looked as though it housed the head of a freakish, one-eyed gladiator.

Pet shut its eye in defeat, and the helmet prison went black.

45. A Drop in the Bucket

Edgar dangled Pet inches above Morella. Her little jaws snapped with the frenzy of a bulldog.

"Treacherous wig!" growled Edgar. "You're so quick to drop your toxic tears into my sister's food—to change her into some kind of monster—well, where are your tears *now*?"

Pet shivered, and the ends of its hair curled ever so slightly upward, out of harm's way. The plant below sensed the promise of a very big *something* for dinner, and it lunged with all its might.

"I know the balm makes *Nepenthes* grow. You absorb the balm, so your tears are some kind of superbalm, aren't they?"

Pet shook from side to side.

Edgar lowered Pet closer to the hungry plant.

"Don't bother lying! You'll be Morella's dinner unless I see you bawling like Mayor Knightleigh at an empty buffet table."

Pet thrashed, and its eye shone with genuine fear. Still, it produced no tears.

Morella coiled like a cobra. Then, launching herself to her full height, the plant clamped her jaws into Pet's hairy middle.

"AIIIIIEEEEEEEEEEE!"

The shriek was needle sharp—and it came from Pet. It was the first sound Edgar had ever heard the creature make.

"Pet!" cried Edgar. "No, no, Morella. Let go. Let go!"

Edgar tugged Pet away from the plant. A single tear seeped out of the big yellow eye, and as it splashed into Morella's open jaws, Edgar saw that the little nub—the baby seed—had broken off somewhere inside the hairball.

"Are you all right, Pet?" asked Edgar. "Oh, cripes. I didn't mean to do that."

Edgar placed Pet gently on the floor. It winced, then slunk toward the door.

"That must have, um, really hurt," said Edgar. He rubbed the back of his neck, then scratched his chin. "I mean, we've put you through a lot over the years and, well…you've never…*yelped* before. I—I'm sorry."

Pet shuffled slowly out of the greenhouse without looking back. Its movements looked pained.

For her part, Morella had stopped her snapping and was as still as a proper plant.

Edgar ran after Pet, but the animal would not be caught a second time. Eventually Edgar returned to the greenhouse. The storm had ended and a brilliant moon had broken through the clouds. In the eerie glow, Morella's mouth seemed strange—wider than before, and deeper. Something inside reflected the moonlight.

Seeds.

46. Misery Loves Company

"Stephanie!" Judith shouted as she strode to the limousine. "Where is Ellen? We need to be at the mansion in fifteen minutes. Enrique and the crew will be there at eight on the dot." She got in next to her daughter, and the chauffeur started the limousine.

"Miles said she raced home before the sun came up," Stephanie answered. The limo drove through the front gate of Knightleigh Manor and turned down Copenhagen Lane toward the twins' house.

"But why?"

"Maybe she missed her coffin."

"What was that?" asked Judith.

"Uh, coughing. She was coughing all night and probably just needed some throat drops."

"Well, she'd better not be hoarse on camera," Judith said coldly as the tower mansion and its now beautifully landscaped yard came into view. "Ah, here we are. It's a shame there wasn't time to install the helicopter pad on the roof. *That* would have been an entrance."

The limousine rolled to a stop, and the chauffeur opened the car door. Stephanie took her time climbing out.

"Turn the limo around and keep the motor running, Boyles," she said. "I want a quick escape route."

As Judith followed her out and smoothed her peach suit jacket, a second and slightly longer limousine pulled up behind hers.

"Rico!" Judith shouted.

Enrique Villalobos, nationally adored host of *Better Homes Than Yours*, opened the limousine door and roared.

"Judith! Stainsworth! Knightleigh!"

Judith and Enrique exchanged air kisses.

"How fabulous to see you again, Rico. You look marvelous!"

"Yes, I do. Now, Judith," purred the man, "this had better not be a waste of my time. From out here, your 'mind-boggling renovation' looks like a dilapidated gray spike—which makes me think of the *downward* spike in my ratings if I show this heap to my audience."

"We've only just begun," Judith said, leading the host by the arm toward the house. "The yard was a biohazard before my top-notch landscaping crew took over. Now it rivals the grounds of our own Knight-lorian Hotel."

"But the exterior of the house, Judith—"

"You want to show the outside? Film the hotel and use that instead," Judith said. "You can do anything. You're on television."

"Ah, not only that, Judith," said Enrique Villalobos, flashing the brilliant smile that made him the world's most beloved renovation show host. "I *am* television."

"Now that's the Rico I adore!" Judith squeezed his arm. "When you see what we've done with the ball-room, I just know you will fall in love with the place."

Enrique stopped abruptly at the entrance, studying the word carved above it.

"My dear," he began, "have you noticed this? It says 'schadenfreude' over the door!"

"Yes, charming period detail, isn't it?"

"Do you have any idea what that means?"

"Er," said Judith, "a family name, perhaps?"

"It means 'pleasure derived from the misery of others.' A little disturbing, don't you think?"

"Perhaps your translation is inaccurate, Rico. You will find only joy inside this home."

47. Light Reading

Once Edgar had ground Morella's seeds into a paste, he still had two big problems.

First, he had enough for only one dose. Second, he could not simply march in and shove the paste into Ellen's mouth. Wary of a potential last-minute strike, Stephanie had instructed the work crews to place guards at the door of the ballroom.

"Aye, fair maiden," Sir Malvolio had assured Stephanie. "Nary a pale, pajama-bedecked knave shall enter."

"We'll put our best man on it, little lady," declared Officer Strongbowe.

Edgar overheard the whole exchange and stole down to the library, where the day before Judith and Ellen had discussed colors for the new home theater. The magazines they had consulted still sat on the desk: *Perfect Living*, *Better Mansions and Estates*, *Country Charm for the Urban Walk-Up*, *Urban Chic for the Country Getaway*—each one chock full of ideas for the high-society entertainer and well-to-do hostess.

Edgar swiped the whole stack. He sped through articles and pictures, ripping out pages. He stopped at a lavish picture of a peacock sculpted from zucchini. A wide smile spread across his face, the first in days.

"Bon appétit," he said.

48. Send in the Clown

Edgar emerged from the kitchen minutes later, wearing a pilfered powder blue catering jacket. He carried a plate covered with an upside-down pasta strainer, an amusing notion he had picked up from page 67 of *Appetizers Digest*. Whistling cheerily, he climbed the stairs to the ballroom.

Stationed at the entrance, Sir Geoffrey and Nathan Ruby griped about being volunteered for guard duty while the rest of their crews mingled with the popular television host and snacked on tasty hors d'oeuvres.

"Look at this honkin' blister," whined Nathan Ruby, showing Sir Geoffrey his thumb. "Weed-whacked that darn yard for five hours straight."

"Oh, yeah?" Sir Geoffrey pulled down his lower lip. "Chipped two of my bottom teeth opening a paint can!"

Edgar took a deep breath and forced a smile as he approached the two men. "Cheerio, gentlemen! May I pass and bring nourishment to our guests?"

Sir Geoffrey let his lip go with a smack and eyed Edgar suspiciously.

"We're not supposed to let anybody else in here," he said. "Chip...I mean, Malvolio said we were on the lookout for a, uh, *roguish churl.*"

Edgar shook his head impatiently.

"Gentlemen," he said. "Would a churl make a delicacy like this?" Edgar lifted the strainer to give the guards a peek.

Nathan Ruby raised an eyebrow. "Rich folks sure do like weird food."

"Exactly," said Edgar, slamming the strainer back onto the plate. "Mrs. Stainsworth-Knightleigh specifically requested that I make a plate of my special treats for the host of the show. She'd be awfully angry if she heard you didn't let me in."

"Uh, maybe, but…" began Sir Geoffrey.

"So let me pass. If I see this churl of yours, I'll tell him you're looking for him."

"Well, that's sure helpful of you," said Sir Geoffrey.

Nathan Ruby looked around, and then leaned in close to Edgar.

"Will you bring us back a couple of those yummy eee-clairs?" he asked. "Those are my favorite."

"Cream puffs for me! Three! I want three of those puppies!" Sir Geoffrey licked his lips.

Edgar slipped past the hungry guards with his plate.

"*Eee-clairs* and *cream puffs*," he said. "Very good."

Edgar padded into the crowded ballroom. He darted in and out of small clusters of crew workers and camera people, constantly on the lookout for Stephanie.

Edgar placed the plate next to a spread of sugary pastries on a new Victorian buffet table, and he artfully folded several paper towels into flowers (*Cottage and Carriage House,* page 32).

He jumped when Judith's voice boomed above the din in the room.

"WHERE IS ELLEN?"

A voice boomed back.

"HERE I AM!"

The entire room froze when Ellen twirled into the ballroom.

"Don't I look pretty?"

Ellen's cheeks, covered in rouge, glowed like two stoplights. Dark mascara coated her lashes in sickening clumps, though her eyes themselves were red from jabbing herself with the mascara wand. She'd smothered her lips and, inadvertently, her teeth with pink lipstick.

As a final touch, Ellen had curled her hair with the curling iron Judith had given her. Wisps of smoke rose from her head.

Everyone was too aghast to speak.

"Wh-what have you done to yourself?" Judith finally stammered.

"Don't you like it?"

"Is that your face under there?" Stephanie asked.

"It is dramatic, isn't it?"

"If a circus clown is dramatic, yes," said Stephanie.

"Ellen will not go on LIVE television looking like DEATH!" Judith demanded as she gripped Ellen's arm. "Stephanie! Come!" And with that, she pulled Ellen from the room. Stephanie followed, unable to hide a smirk.

Enrique Villalobos, oblivious to the commotion, clapped his hands.

"Let's get ready, people! Ten minutes to show time!"

49. Twists and Turnips

Ellen came back into the room a few minutes later, her face clean and rather pinkish from Judith's scouring. Draped over her pajamas was Stephanie's lavender suit jacket. Judith insisted Ellen wear it to cover "that ridiculous unitard," despite Stephanie's protests.

Ellen spied her brother lurking by the buffet table in his caterer's coat, and she skipped over to him.

"What do you have there, Edgar?"

"Oh, just a little something I whipped up. I'm not sure it's any good. I'm almost embarrassed to put it out."

"How thoughtful! See how pleasant it is to be pleasant?"

"Indeed. The last few days have made me sick to my stomach."

"Think no more of it. Let's see this masterpiece!" Ellen exclaimed.

Edgar removed the pasta strainer with a flourish.

Ellen squealed loudly, and several of the television crew came over for a look.

On the plate sat twelve halved turnips carved rather crudely to resemble peacocks. Their hollowed-out bodies held a lumpy, grainy mixture that looked like wet oatmeal and diced olives. Ellen applauded.

"It's nothing fancy," said Edgar. "Something I picked up from this month's *Suburban Sophisticate*. Modified it just a tad. It's a ca-NAPE."

"You mean cana-PAY," said Ellen, correctly pronouncing the appetizer.

"Just *eat* one," said Edgar.

The assembled crowd did not respond to Edgar's invitation. Except for Ellen. She snatched a peacock and took a bite.

"Oh! Exquisite," she cooed.

"I think you'll find *this* one even *tastier*," said Edgar, holding out a poorly carved peacock that seemed to sprout horns.

"Let's make sure there's enough for everyone first," said Ellen. She offered the plate to a man holding cue cards.

"Oh, sure," he said as he picked up a peacock and bit into it. "Well, I'll be! This ca-*NAPE* is none too shabby!"

Members of the TV crew looked at one another, then took peacocks of their own. While not everyone gave such happy squeals, they mumbled appreciative words like "engaging" and "inventive fusion of flavors."

"What's going on here?" said Stephanie, pushing through the snackers. "YOU!" She pointed a finger at Edgar. "I told those idiots to keep you out of here. Those ugly pajamas of yours will double nicely as a prison uniform. *Security!*" She strode off in search of her guards.

"Please, Ellen," said Edgar urgently, and he again pushed the horned turnip, the last one remaining, toward his sister. She eyed it hungrily, but Judith stepped between them.

"Oh, thank goodness. I need some small sustenance, and all the caterers brought were sugars and starches."

She plucked the last turnip from the tray.

"No, that's not yours!" shouted Edgar.

"Brother! So rude," said Ellen. "Please don't mind him, Mrs. Stainsworth-Knightleigh."

"I never would," said Judith. She turned the turnip left and right, sizing it up.

Edgar coughed.

"Um, um, ah—fat," he said.

"Excuse me, Egbert?" asked Judith.

"Fat—fatty, fatty—FAT," he cried. "The secret ingredient is, is…Macedonia nuts. Which is one of the lard-based nuts, you know. Full of *fat.*"

Judith's thin eyebrows arched.

"Just thought you'd like to know," Edgar continued. "What's a gourmet meal without a ladle-full of fat, I always say."

Judith discreetly slipped the peacock back to the plate.

"What are we doing, people?" Enrique Villalobos shouted. "Places! We go live in two minutes!"

Judith wiped her hands with one of the flower-shaped napkins. "I suggest we avoid rich foods right now. It will only lead to bloat and drifting attention spans."

She clacked back across the room toward the cameras, leaving Edgar unattended with his sister.

Edgar relaxed his fists.

"Fat content doesn't concern you, of course," he said to Ellen. "You need some meat on your bones."

"Oh, Edgar, I couldn't."

"What *now*?"

"It's the last one. It's rude to eat the last thing on a plate. Judith says that the polite thing to do is to leave it for someone else."

"That someone else is you!" yelled Edgar. Out of the corner of his eye he spied Stephanie across the room berating her guards and pointing at him.

Ellen patted Edgar sweetly on the cheek and turned to take her place under the lights. Edgar's brow furrowed.

"I seasoned it with *cinnamon*, Sister, just because I know how much you like it. It would break my heart if you didn't eat it."

Ellen paused and looked over her shoulder.

"Cinnamon?"

She glanced around to see if anyone was watching. Edgar held the treat out to tempt her.

"Well, I wouldn't want to upset you...."

Edgar pouted and threw in a couple of sniffles. Across the room, an angry painter and lawn officer were coming his way.

Ellen reached for the treat, but as she put it to her lips, a one-eyed mass of hair landed on her head.

"What the—?" Ellen dropped the peacock in confusion, and Pet's single eye twitched madly, taunting Edgar. The creature's oily locks covered Ellen's eyes, and it cracked several of them at Edgar like whips.

"No, no, fiend!" hissed Edgar. "I've uncovered your crafty scheme, and your play for revenge shall end!"

Edgar leapt at his sister, yanked Pet off her head, and threw it to the ground.

"Yes, the wig was a bad idea," said a nearby cameraman as the hairball spun across the ballroom floor.

Ellen staggered forward, nearly trodding on the turnip, but Edgar snatched it up and shoved it into her mouth, just as two sets of hands took him by the arms.

"Eat up!"

50. Showtime

Sir Geoffrey and Nathan Ruby dragged Edgar to the back of the ballroom as a battalion of bulbs flared to life. Twenty or so people snapped to attention behind their video cameras, microphones, and official-looking clipboards in preparation for the day's filming. The bright lights exposed every nook of the ballroom, and for the first time Edgar took note of the room's extensive transformation.

Plush armchairs and mahogany-stained accent tables showed richly against the white marble floor. Upon the tables sat collections of china dolls, plates, and other expensive-looking baubles. Orange lightbulbs shaped like flames flickered atop decorative brass candlesticks.

Gilt-framed mirrors lined the walls, interspersed with portraits of historic Nod's Limbsians (all Knightleighs). In the center of the room the chandelier sparkled, its teardrop crystals polished to utter brilliance.

Enrique Villalobos strode to Ellen's side as she choked down the last of her canapé.

"Ellen, my lovely, when the cameras roll, I'm going to introduce this resplendent manor using my trademark baritone. Then I will motion to you. That's your cue to say your line, which is…?"

Ellen responded faintly, "Thank you, Enrique, and what a joy it is to have you in our humble home."

"Hmm, yes," said Enrique Villalobos. "Though you could give it a little more pep."

Ellen nodded stiffly.

"Ready, chief?" asked a man wearing a headset.

"Burt," said Enrique Villalobos, "I was born ready."

Judith scooted a candelabra a quarter-inch to the right, then gave Ellen some final words of encouragement. "Don't be nervous, don't frown, and don't embarrass me."

Burt spun and shouted to the crew. "Remember people, *live* means no second chances! And five… four…three…"

He counted the last two beats on his fingers, then pointed at Enrique Villalobos. On cue, the host unleashed a powerful white smile and winked. He opened his arms wide and spoke in deep, comforting tones.

> *Hello, house-lovers, and welcome to another edition of* Better Homes Than Yours! *Fixer-Upper Week continues LIVE at this stunning neo-post-quasi-Colonial mansion in the lovely town of Nod's Limbs. What began as a faded jewel from yesteryear has undergone a magnificent transformation under the watchful eye of well-known domestic diva Judith Stainsworth-Knightleigh. We'll talk more with the Queen of Clean herself later, but first let's meet our hostess, the delightful Miss Ellen.*

Enrique Villalobos gestured to the pale girl, and the camera panned down. Ellen's pointy face filled the dozen or so little TV monitors set up around the room.

Ellen didn't respond.

"What's the matter with her?" whispered Stephanie.

"Uh, Ellen, what a kind gesture to let us into your home," Enrique Villalobos said.

Ellen shuddered and seemed surprised to find that someone was talking to her.

"Oh, uh, thank you, Enrique," said Ellen faintly. "And what a...what a *joy*—"

Ellen gagged. She clutched her throat and gasped for air.

Burt looked up from his camera.

Enrique picked up the lag.

"Why don't you tell us a bit about where we're standing now? In its heyday this was a grand ballroom. How do you plan to use it after it has been restored?"

Ellen's entire body quaked, but still she did not speak. Judith clicked her tongue and was about to walk on camera to save the situation, when a screech shattered the air.

It came from Ellen.

"I'll tell you how I plan to use it," she cried. "I plan to bring it down around your ears, you pompous,

primetime hack!" She ripped off the lavender jacket and threw it into the host's face.

The room fell silent, save for one voice that piped up from the rear.

"Welcome back, Sister!"

51. Sister Dearest

Ellen seized the nearest object: a bowl of cranberry punch.

"You look parched, Rico! How about some refreshment?" she yelled as she doused the host with the ruby liquid.

Enrique shrieked, and Ellen flipped over a replica Louis XIV coffee table, hitting him in the knees. He staggered backward and tangled himself in a forest of microphone stands.

Next, Ellen yanked the window drapes, pulling the curtain rods down with them. Chunks of plaster fell like hail.

Sirs Gionello and Horatio dove at Ellen, trying to restrain her, but Ellen threw the drapes over them. The two men blundered past and crashed into Wesley Puddlesby, who was closing in on Ellen from behind.

Wesley knocked over a tower of TV lights, shattering the bulbs in a *pop-pop-popping* explosion.

The television crew tried to escape, but the fallen light tower blocked the stairwell.

Ellen kicked candelabras and stomped on their flame-shaped bulbs. She swept a collection of imitation Venetian vases off a sidetable, but rather than shatter, the phony urns bounced across the marble, tripping the still-draped Gionello and Horatio.

In the center of the storm, Burt calmly manned his camera. Ellen's rampage appeared on dozens of monitors in the room—as well as on millions of TV sets around the country.

Into the frame marched Judith Stainsworth-Knightleigh, followed by Stephanie.

"M–m–my *ballroom*," she stammered. "Why are you…getting it…*dirty*?"

"I told you, Mother!" called Stephanie. "She waited for our big moment to betray us!" She charged at Ellen, who was bashing accent tables with one of the curtain rods. "I've been waiting to do this all week, you miserable freak!"

At that moment, Edgar finally wrestled free from Nathan Ruby and Sir Geoffrey and nabbed a plate of pastries. He pummeled Stephanie with éclair after éclair.

"Don't talk with your mouth full, Stephanie!" Edgar jeered.

Ellen, meanwhile, climbed up one of the remaining light towers and jumped onto the chandelier in the center of the room. She swung by one arm, using her free hand to pluck teardrop crystals and hurl them at the crowd below.

Blinded by rage and pastry filling, Stephanie leapt off a table and caught hold of Ellen's dangling ankle. The chandelier swayed, its mad arc made wilder by the struggling girls. The support beams in the ceiling splintered and began to give way, and the chandelier dropped several feet.

The crowd at the blocked stairwell grew frantic; Officer Dwight Strongbowe and Sir Malvolio desperately tried to move the light tower aside, but were prevented by the people trying to push past. Only Judith Stainsworth-Knightleigh seemed oblivious to the threat of the looming chandelier. She unsuccessfully grabbed at her daughter's feet.

"Stephanie!" shouted Judith. "Get that savage down NOW!"

Burt deftly moved his camera, alternately filming the cowering crowd and the frenzied girls, who now swung across the room like battling trapeze artists. Enrique Villalobos crawled under the buffet table.

Then Jill Geronimo noticed something the rest of the room did not.

"There are pipes running above that ceiling, old ones," she shouted to the others. "Somebody should get those girls down before—"

CRRRACK! The chandelier dropped another two feet and more plaster crumbled from the ceiling, revealing a particularly rusty pipe. A small stream of water trickled from it.

"I knew you'd ruin this!" Stephanie shouted. "I never fell for your game!"

Ellen lifted her knee to her chest. "Never fell, you say?"

She kicked Stephanie's shoulder, and the girl lost her grip and dropped onto her mother. The two Knightleighs fell into a bowl of fish dip. Ellen flew off the chandelier on the backswing, plowing into Officer Strongbowe.

The rusty pipe rumbled like a woeful whale. The painters stopped fumbling with the light tower, and the crowd turned slowly as a few drops of water hit the marble floor and the cords of the chandelier began to snap. For a second, no one moved.

"Run away!" screamed Sir Malvolio. But there was no escape.

The chandelier plummeted and landed with a deafening crash that sent hundreds of crystal teardrops in all directions. The pipe ruptured and a gush of filthy water poured into the ballroom.

In moments everyone was slipping, sliding, and falling across the floor. Enrique Villalobos flailed on his back like a helpless turtle.

The water rushed down the stairs, taking with it light towers, teardrop crystals, imitation vases, and Judith's reputation. The TV crew picked up any broadcast equipment that wasn't hissing or smoking and made for the exit. The Lawn and Order team did their best to guide (or, in some cases, glide) Jill Geronimo, Wesley Puddlesby, and the rest of the crowd to safety. Burt alone stayed at his post, faithfully capturing the mayhem for audiences nationwide.

Ellen saw Judith and Stephanie wobbling precariously toward the staircase. She seized a corner of newly applied wallpaper and wrenched it from the wall. The cascading sheet of gooey, gluey paper swallowed the Knightleighs, rolling them up like spider's silk around a fly. They pushed and screeched inside their paper prison.

"Save the damsels!" cried Sir Malvolio, and Sirs Horatio and Gionello hefted the Knightleighs over

their shoulders and bore them downstairs, slipping and sliding as they went. Sir Geoffrey shoved three water-logged cream puffs into his tunic and followed after.

"Put me down, you oafs!" Judith barked. "I have a show to do! We're not finished here! Places, people!"

"Do you believe me *now*, Mother?" bellowed Stephanie.

Burt turned off his camera and leaned back.

"That was the best show we've ever done."

He stepped gingerly toward the stairs.

"You coming, Rico?"

Enrique Villalobos, television host extraordinaire, cowered underneath the buffet table,.

"Is it over, Burt? Is it really over?"

"It's over, Rico. Time to hit the road."

The bewildered television personality, now drenched in filthy water, plaster, and punch, crawled from beneath the table. He scrambled through the puddles on hands and knees and fled down the stairs, mumbling, "Schadenfreude, schadenfreude."

The driving flow from the pipe slowed to a gentle stream. Ellen wrung one of the sleeves of her drenched pajamas. "Guess that's a wrap, Brother."

> *Our guests, so quick to disappear,*
> *Distressed by plunging chandelier,*
> *Left only crashing crystal tears*
> *To weep for Judith's lost career.*
> *It proves what we've known from the start,*
> *That mischief is an ingrained art—*
> *It lives inside our rascally hearts*
> *That plot together, not apart.*
> *The moral of this morning's fun?*
> *Two prankish minds work best as one!*

52. In Time of War

"It was the strangest thing," said Ellen. "Like I was trapped inside my body, not able to get out, not able to control my actions. I felt…happy and…*wholesome.*"

"It was terrible to watch," said Edgar. "Do you remember much?"

"No—I mean, it's coming back slowly. I—I—I wore lip gloss?" Ellen shuddered.

"That's not the worst of it."

"What could be wor—Edgar! I slept at Stephanie Knightleigh's house last night!"

"You wore her pajamas."

"Oh, those Knightleighs are going to pay for what they did to me—and to our house!" Ellen pointed to the shredded damask slipcovers on the floor.

"To our house, yes," said Edgar. "But they weren't the ones responsible for your...er...transformation."

"What do you mean?"

"It was Pet."

"*Pet?* How could it—"

"You've missed a lot, Sister," said Edgar, and he explained the events of the past week.

Ellen collapsed into a soaked armchair. "So, Morella was my savior!"

"In a way, yes," said Edgar. "But the important thing is that *Pet* is an entirely different creature than we thought. Smart. Cunning. Wicked."

"A worthy adversary, perhaps?"

"Or maybe even...an ally?"

53. History Repeats

"Until we know for sure what Pet's motives are, we should restrict its movement," said Ellen, pulling on a pigtail. "I don't want it crying on me while I sleep."

"Good idea. I'll disable the dumbwaiter. You reinforce the lab entrance," said Edgar.

The dumbwaiter box hung in the library. Wielding a screwdriver, Edgar wedged one arm inside the small elevator and began to take the box apart.

As he worked, he spied some writing on the platform of the box. It appeared to be burned into the wood:

To Pilos—

May you ride in comfort all the days of your long, long life.

Augustus

1799

"More of Nod's handiwork, I suppose. But where have I heard the name Pilos before?" Edgar said. He straightened up and cracked his knuckles.

Ellen entered the library carrying a tattered book.

"I've been looking through the diary," she announced. "I wanted to find out more about the balm, and I stumbled across a strange entry—"

"That's it!" shouted Edgar. "Pilosoculus!"

"Yes, Pilosoculus. How did you know?"

"Pilos—Augustus Nod built this dumbwaiter for someone named Pilos. It must be short for Pilosoculus. I remembered it from the journal, but I have no idea who Pilos is—must have been a pretty small person to fit in this elevator."

"Edgar, listen to *this*."

Ellen opened the diary and began to read aloud:

The Balm consumes me, and this has led to a most disturbing antagonism with Pilosoculus. I would do anything for the creature, but it will not explain its reasoning, and frankly, I find it troublesome that it should want to deny me the extraordinary wholesomeness the Balm provides. Does it hoard it for itself? Bah, I do not wish to believe it. And yet, I cannot be sure of the motives that lie beneath its hairy exterior... Pilos would seem to do anything to keep me from the spring...

"That's the end of the entry. Nod was afraid of this *Pilos*," said Ellen.

Edgar looked at the dumbwaiter inscription again.

"*Hairy*...It can't be," he murmured. "But the name sounds...it sounds like..."

He began searching through the piles of books scattered about the library and pulled out a thick, dusty tome:

DEAD LANGUAGES LIVE:
Latin to English Dictionary

Edgar flipped to the *P* section.

"Pilatus...Pilleatus...," he read. "Here we go: 'Pilosus, *Covered in hair.*'"

He thumbed back to the *O*s.

"Octoni...Octuplus...Oculus," he read in a trembling voice. *"The eyeball."*

Ellen dropped the journal.

"Pilosoculus means…the hairy eyeball?" she gasped. "Pet? Our Pet? But that would mean it's over two hundred years old."

"Why not?" said Edgar, "Anything's possible where Pet is concerned."

"What if Pet betrayed Nod? What if it's responsible for his disappearance? It may do the same to us!"

A squeak came from the stairs, and Edgar and Ellen spun around to see hundreds of beady eyes staring back at them. It was the largest pack of rats they had ever seen, as if the entire rat population of Nod's Limbs were holding a convention on their stairwell.

And at the top of the horde was Pet.

54. Downward Spiral

The twins stared, unsure what to do next.

Pet was not so indecisive.

The ball of hair nodded its eye ever so slightly, and the rats surged together, sweeping into the library in a wave of fur and tails.

Before Edgar and Ellen could respond, rats were swarming about and over them, until the twins were pulled to the ground on top of the furry mob.

"What's going on?" Ellen shouted over the squeals of the rodents.

"Hey—I can't get up," said Edgar. "They—they won't let me go!"

The long, leathery tails wrapped like shackles around hands, feet, and pigtails. Sharp teeth seized folds in the twins' pajamas, and a writhing cushion of rodents carried their bodies forth.

Edgar wriggled fiercely but could not wrest free. He caught a glimpse of his sister tumbling over the edge of the steps. Riding the rodents like a skittery magic carpet, Edgar felt his own legs follow, then his torso, and finally his head, down, down, down, flight after flight of stairs.

The rats were not gentle, and the twins found their heads and limbs bumping against each step along the way.

Down and down and down, past the kitchen, the parlor, the front hall, and into the basement.

"Where"—*thwack*—"are they"—*thwack*—"taking" —*thwack*—"us?"—*thwack*—"*Ouch!*" Ellen shouted up at her brother as they entered the subbasement.

"At least we're at the end of the line!" Edgar called out.

But he was wrong.

55. Breakthrough

No stairs remained, but the rats streamed toward the giant wine cask that hid the entrance to the underground lab. As usual, the door was shut and locked fast.

The rats sped at the cask; the twins were powerless to stop them.

CRASH!

Edgar and Ellen smashed into the barrel, feet first. The ancient wood buckled and shattered with the impact, and splinters rained. The rats loosened their grip and the twins came free, toppling head over heels down the staircase and landing in a heap at the bottom. They could hear scurrying and squealing as the last of the rat army scrambled over them and into the darkness; then all was silent.

Ellen groaned.

"Brother? Are we dead?"

"No, not dead," Edgar replied. "Unless rodents are guides to the afterlife."

"I feel like the underside of a shoe," said Ellen, pushing herself up. "What happened?"

"We got hijacked by a pack of rats who used us as a battering ram," Edgar said.

"I recall," said Ellen. "But Pet launched the charge."

"We need light, Sister. Pet could be lurking around here planning another attack!"

They scrambled toward the electric generator. Ellen fumbled with the handle and began to crank. The antique bulbs flickered on, and the twins saw hundreds of rodent tracks leading into the cavern, but no sign of the hairy eyeball.

"It was hungry for more balm," Edgar said. "The bit we fed it in the greenhouse gave it the strength to pull all this off—to get back to the source."

"And it used us to do it, as if we were nothing but tools." Ellen's voice betrayed a hint of admiration.

56. The Belly of the Beast

"Brother, it's time to make a truce with Pet. It is a creature after our own hearts—it could even prove a useful assistant in our schemes!"

The twins scoured the lab, rummaging among scientific gadgetry and wooden crates. It was Edgar who saw movement in the dark cavern beyond the halo of the electric lights: a reflective shimmer, like the eyes of a raccoon. A one-eyed raccoon, perhaps.

"Out there! By the pit!"

"The pit? Is Pet going to throw itself in?"

Pet slunk along the edge of a dark abyss. During the hunt for the Mason, Edgar himself had almost fallen in the very same hole. For all the twins knew, it was bottomless.

"Pet's not jumping in—it's escaping!" cried Ellen.

The twins dashed after it but quickly realized something peculiar: Pet was not heading for the exit that led to the city sewers. Instead, its destination seemed to be a slim opening in the wall that led to a winding honeycomb of caves.

"Why is it headed that way?" whispered Edgar. "That's the path to Heimertz's shed."

Only once had the twins explored the twisting tunnel that led to a trapdoor beneath the caretaker's shed. After a close brush with Heimertz inside his shack, once had proven enough.

"I don't like this," said Ellen. "Whatever it has planned, we need to talk to it *first*."

The twins followed Pet into the tunnel, zigging and zagging toward the trapdoor. They slowed as they drew closer to the dead end.

"Careful," said Edgar. "Don't let Heimertz hear our footsteps."

"Or your heavy breathing," said Ellen, jabbing Edgar's ribs.

Just ahead, lingering on a ledge beneath the trapdoor, was Pet. It sat quietly, illuminated by beams of light that filtered through the floorboards of the shed.

"Hey, Pet. That was a pretty good gag you pulled," Ellen whispered as she crept closer. "Terrific work. We're even, eh? Now let's go back and talk about—"

She was reaching to scoop up the creature when a creak above made her freeze.

Light flooded the tunnel. Heimertz's head leaned in, eyeing first the little creature, then Ellen's stricken

face. Pet, however, did not run or wince or cower—instead it stretched up on the tips of its hairs.

A giant gloved hand reached down, clasped Pet, and pulled it upward. The twins could not move, but their gaze followed Heimertz's hand until they were staring straight at his face. Ellen summoned all her courage to protest.

"Don't—don't you hurt—" She stopped as Heimertz gently placed Pet on his shoulder. Pet winked, and Heimertz slammed the trapdoor shut.

57. The New Agenda

"And *then* she *ripped* the gold leaf wallpaper *right off the walls!*" Judith fumed, pacing the topmost balcony of the Knightlorian Hotel and glaring at the dark house next door. "Gold leaf made with *real gold*, I might add."

"Sounds expensive," said Mayor Knightleigh. "Do you think it can be salvaged?"

"Not a shred of it! Let's just hope I can salvage my *career* after that disaster," Judith said. "How humiliating—in front of *Enrique Villalobos*. In front of *millions of viewers!*"

Just then, Judith heard her own voice screaming from the television set inside. Miles was watching cartoons in the suite, but a news flash showing the day's debacle interrupted the program. Judith stormed into the room. In front of them for the second time that day was Ellen's handiwork: a bedraggled Enrique, the demolished ballroom, and, in the midst of it all, Judith and Stephanie wrapped in gold leaf wallpaper.

Judith slammed her fist on the remote and the screen went black.

"I told you, Mother," said Stephanie. "That girl is not to be trusted. She lures you in, and then she ruins you."

"Enough, Stephanie!" shouted Judith. "If you had been keeping an eye on her like I had asked, this never would have happened!"

Stephanie scowled.

The mayor coughed. "You know what they say, my dear, 'If at first you don't succeed…'"

"Oh, I *will* succeed," said Judith. She strode back out onto the balcony and pointed at the twins' home. "That horror of a house *will not* sully the Knight-lorian's view."

"What do you have in mind?" asked Stephanie.

"Those twins," said Judith, "are children, and they have no known parents."

"Yes, that's right! Both the house and the twins fall to the welfare of the town," said Mayor Knightleigh.

"And as mayor, I have free rein to do what is necessary for the good of Nod's Limbs."

Stephanie examined her parents. "And that means?"

Judith glared at the twins' dark mansion, and a look of deep satisfaction came to her face.

"It means good riddance to that house and the miserable children who live there."

THE END

READ ON FOR A SNEAK
PREVIEW OF THE
TERRIBLE TWINS' NEXT
ADVENTURE:
HIGH WIRE

Willkommen

Nod's Limbs, 1807

"Cursed dwelling! Let dawn see you nothing more than a heap of ashes!" With mad intensity, Pierre Knightleigh struck flint on steel, sending sparks raining on the towering mansion's front steps. "Burn, burn, burn, I say!"

"Steady, sir," said a manservant, standing patiently at the bottom of the steps. "Perhaps you might rest in the carriage and reconsider."

"Confound it, Robbins! Don't you see? They're all *dead*. It's the only way...the only way to rid myself of the curse. I *must* burn it!"

"Please reconsider, sir," said Robbins.

Pierre redoubled his efforts to set the steps alight, muttering all the while:

Nod built himself a dank, gray house,
Went mad as any a Bedlam mouse,
Then disappeared, and there bestowed
Upon me this most foul abode.
Hee hee!

Robbins cleared his throat. "If I may say so, sir, your recent tragedies are what trouble you, not this house. Your father's disappearance—"

"Never to be spoken of!" barked Pierre. "Never! The citizens of Nod's Limbs have been told Thaddeus Knightleigh died in his sleep, and they believe it." He turned his burning eyes to his manservant.

If you're smart, you'll think it, too,
For mayors don't vanish—madmen do.

Pierre paused in his ditty. "But Robbins, I am both mayor *and* madman! Ho ho! Will I vanish like the rest?"

"Allow me to suggest that keeping this secret is contributing to your condition, sir—"

"What condition? *Look out for the camels!*" shrieked Pierre, jumping to his feet and pointing at the clouds. Then he sighed. "No, it was only a flock of weasels."

Robbins did not flinch. "A relief, indeed, sir. But if

I may be so bold, the house can't be blamed for your father's, ah, passing, nor your wife's death."

Pierre dropped the flint and buried his head in his hands. "O, sweet Agatha...first your mother," he paused, and his voice turned bitter, "then your father, the *great* Augustus Nod...but why you? Why so young?" He turned to his manservant. "She grew up here, Robbins. This is where the curse was wrought. She watched her father fall under the house's spell, toiling, toiling, naught but toiling, day and night. It must burn!"

"The house is innocent, sir."

"Ah, but the house *isn't* innocent." Pierre leaned in close and spoke almost below hearing. "There are things in the basement. Unnatural things. Deep below ground..."

Robbins's eyes grew wide despite himself, and Pierre began to sing again.

> *Sighs and groans and piteous moans,*
> *What lies beneath the pebbles and stones?*

"It's the secret, Robbins," he whispered. "The mystical ingredient Nod put in his famous candles."

"The Waxworks candles?" breathed Robbins. "Like

the Nigh-Everlasting Candle? The Vigor-Vapoured Taper? The Flambeau of Felicity?"

"The same," said Pierre. "The candles that earned him mountains of gold—the very stuff that gave those candles their power was wrought by devilry in the bowels of this house."

Robbins took off his tri-cornered hat and waved cool air over his face. "But we are men of the nineteenth century, sir. You cannot mean that you believe in witchcraft?"

"Boo-dilly, ba-dilly, tra-la-la-lilly," Pierre burbled. "Just like the money, you know."

"I beg your pardon, sir?"

"My inheritance is tainted, too. Nod disappears, and his wealth passes to his daughter—but alas! She has died before her time, and I, her husband, receive the bounty. Nod lined his pockets through unholy acts, and those same riches now fill the Knightleigh coffers. Have we inherited Nod's curse with them, Robbins, have we?"

The front door of the house creaked, and both men jumped. A stranger stood in the doorway, as tall as Nod but, unlike the town founder, he had a pleasant, amused expression. He wore colorful Bavarian lederhosen and a traditional Tyrolean hat with a peacock feather tucked in the brim. He held what seemed to be an unpowdered wig with a hen's egg atop.

To the men's shock, the egg *blinked*.

"You vish to remove this curse?" asked the stranger in a thick German accent.

"Wh-who the devil are you?" asked Pierre Knight-leigh.

"This house, you are right, is a heavy burden for those who vould own it. I can take such problems avay."

"Who are you?"

"I am a collector of very special properties. If you sell the house to me, you vill atone for the terrible things that have happened here."

"See, sir?" Robbins spoke hopefully. "No need for an inferno. No reason to create further scandal. Sell the house and be done with it."

Pierre remained silent for a long while, his eyes fixed on the strange foreigner. "To whom shall I sign the deed?"

The man gave a smile so wide and eerie that both Pierre and Robbins recoiled.

"My name," he said, "is Sigmund Heimertz."

Read where the mischief begins...

Edgar & Ellen

MISCHIEF & MAYHEM™ GAME

Play pranks and wreak havoc around Nod's Limbs in this darkly humorous board game.

G9136

GLOW-IN-THE-DARK PUZZLE

Piece together Edgar & Ellen's latest misadventure. Their gadgets glow!

H2257

Enjoy Edgar & Ellen?
Add to the adventure at
www.edgarandellen.com!

ENTER THE WONDERFULLY WICKED WORLD OF EDGAR & ELLEN! Become a reporter for the *Nod's Limbs Gazette* and use your byline to share the horrible truth! Write your own mischievous tales star-ing Edgar & Ellen! Watch the cartoon or play the diabolically great games!